STATEWIDE STORIES

Tales of Hometown

Legends & Lore

ANTHOLOGY EDITED BY
BRITTANY TUCKER

FRUIT PRESS

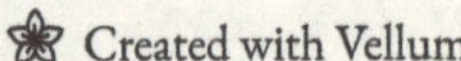 Created with Vellum

NOTE FROM THE EDITOR

BRITTANY TUCKER

There's something so bonding about shared experiences. Whether we've both had our cash eaten by the same vending machine or seen the silhouette of an eight-foot-tall hairy ape-man in the woods, it doesn't matter—experiences bring us together. New or old. Real or fake. Experiences become stories. We'll listen to Grandma tell us the same one a thousand times because it's a way to connect. Connect with her, connect with the past.

With the passage of time, experiences become stories, and stories become legends, passed down from parent to child through the ages until it's a part of who we are, our heritage.

Not only does every country have its native legends, but so do small towns and communities. Something always makes a region special, no matter how small. That's what I wanted this anthology to capture—the legends of *our* hometowns. *Our* lore.

Not only that, but to put our individual spins on our favorite stories. Because stories become legends, those stories must continue to be told to keep those legends alive.

Inside *Statewide Stories,* you'll find fiction tales told by writers from all walks of life—from career authors, to hobbyists, to kids just discovering their passion for writing. I've purposely limited the editing done on the stories submitted by younger writers for authenticity and to highlight the beauty of how our storytelling abilities progress through time and practice.

Reading through every story submitted was such a joy, and I hope you enjoy them as much as I have!

THE TRUTH ABOUT FIRE TRAIL

B.E. PADGETT, WA.

IT WAS A QUIET LEGEND IN TOWN. A SMALL superstition hardly shared in the community—that Fire Trail Road was haunted. A story Lyla never believed because, well . . . ghosts aren't real. And Fire Trail Road wasn't haunted.

She'd watched enough Ghost Inspectors to know that breezes move doors, squeaky pipes sound like spirit-like moans, and people's imaginations were wild. But it wasn't just that the evidence of ghostly encounters was vague and unconvincing that made Lyla a skeptic. It was because she walked Fire Trail Road every morning to the gas station between 3:30–4:30 AM for work every day for the last five years. In all that time, she'd never seen a ghost. Of course, she'd seen other things.

Like cars in ditches. Someone would take the lower turn too fast, or on cold, rainy days, a driver might get mud under their wheels and spin out, diving front-first into the almost overflowing drainage channels. It happened more often than she'd like. Most days, she'd only see the cleanup. But Lyla had once witnessed a terrible accident herself.

A silver SUV had slammed into the bridge railing at high speed, tearing the metal off its wooden planks. The railing had

"

scooted and slid along the asphalt right in front of Lyla on her way to work. The SUV flipped onto its side and into a ditch full of late January showers, layers of mud, and rotten leaves from the winter season.

Lyla didn't remember much about how it happened, just the aftereffects of it as soon as her brain processed what she'd seen. For several minutes, she had stood there staring at the SUV, patting her pockets for her phone. The roads were empty. She needed to call 911. The driver was barely visible and unconscious. The early morning sun was barely enough to see the shape of a passenger on the water-filling side of the vehicle.

Before Lyla realized she didn't have her phone, another car had already pulled over to help. A man with a cellphone pressed tightly between his ear and shoulder jumped. He knocked on the tilted vehicle's door and yelled at the driver. He didn't acknowledge Lyla or ask her what happened. He was all urgent action—everything Lyla was not.

It had been traumatic. But when the man arrived, Lyla was more than relieved. She couldn't stay to talk to the police. She had to get to work. Couldn't be late. Couldn't lose her job over an accident that looked well under control.

When she got off work that day, Lyla was surprised to see that most evidence of the accident was gone. The only things left behind were the crushed metal railing, which sat on the side of the road, and the tire tread marks where the car had been towed out.

Later, Lyla would see the accident in the headlines at the gas station. The driver had been rushed to the hospital and would make a full recovery. Their passenger, an unfortunate hitchhiker, however, did not survive.

That part of the story always stuck out to her. Walking a long road in Washington State, where it rained several months out of the year, hitchhiking was a welcome opportunity for those who didn't have cars. Lyla had done it many times before. If it could cut her commute down, she was more than grateful to the families or truck drivers who'd give her a short lift down the road, especially if the weather was poor.

The last few times, Lyla hadn't had any luck. The older woman who picked her up had immediately pulled over a few blocks later and told her to get out. She wasn't sure what she had done, but she wasn't one for taking rides from frenzied people.

The time before that had been a young commuter. He seemed nice and welcoming at first when Lyla had slipped into the back seat, but after a few minutes on the road, his continuous glancing through the rearview mirror had made her nervous. She'd asked him to stop the car.

Without a word, but with a jaw almost hitting the floor as if offended, the man had let her out a few blocks from the gas station.

It made getting rides hard and uncomfortable, so Lyla tried to avoid it. Cars in ditches and hitchhiking mishaps were the only weird things that ever happened on the road.

No, there had never been ghosts on Fire Trail Road. Not in all the years Lyla walked it.

Not in all the times had she taken it to and from work. She had never seen anything paranormal or believed the stories.

Until now.

Lyla left her house at 3:30 AM. It was dark as winter months usually were. And cold. Not below-zero cold, but cold enough for someone born and raised in the Pacific Northwest. Her usual gloves and coat barely seemed to touch the chill of the wind. She scanned the roadway up and down as she traveled, listening for the engine of a car heading out early for a Seattle or Renton commute. It would be a good day to get a quick ride.

A few blocks into her walk, she heard the sound of a popping engine behind her. Lyla peeked over her shoulder. It was an older truck, almost a classic by the shape of its headlights.

She ripped off her glove and stuck her thumb out, indicating the direction she needed to go, and the truck slowed.

It was Lyla's experience to give the car room to pull over and herself the opportunity to peek at the driver before asking for a ride. The passenger window was manually rolled down. Inside was a handsome couple, both neatly dressed as if heading to a Sunday worship service. In the back seat of the car was a boy, his face turned from her, staring out the driver's side window.

"You need a ride, love?" the woman asked as if Lyla weren't a thirty-something-year-old woman and potentially older than her by several years.

"Yes, thank you. It's not far. The gas station on State?" Lyla studied the family and vehicle. It was an old truck. Old but new-looking. A classic for sure. Lyla was no truck nerd, but she knew four-door trucks from the 1960s were a rarity, but not unheard of.

"Hop on in, we have plenty of room," the man said.

Lyla climbed into the back cab. The seats were slightly worn but looked original and had been well restored to their former glory. It was quiet in the truck except for the radio playing a classic tune Lyla barely recognized as one of her mom's favorites. To break the silence, she said, "Wow, this is a really nice truck. What year is she? 1960?"

"1965 actually." The man smiled through the rearview mirror.

"We just love her, drives like a dream," the woman answered, looking back at her.

"It must have taken a fortune to restore."

"Nah, she was like new when we bought her. I'm Sandy Mills, by the way." She stuck a hand out to Lyla. Her nails were perfectly manicured. They shook hands before she darted her eyes to the boy leaning against the car door. "Don't be rude, Charlie, and say hello to the lady."

Charlie just waved—his face and body turned away from her.

"Hi," he mumbled. Lyla eyed him up and down. He seemed nervous around her. His body hugged his door as far away from her as he could get. Suddenly, Lyra felt self-conscious. Did she stink? Was it how she was dressed?

Lyla didn't dress up for work. A gas station wasn't really a place to wear a dress or get nails done up. She wore clothes that were both comfortable and weather-appropriate. Maybe it was the massive coat she wore, or the gloves that made the kid nervous. Maybe it was her jeans, which hid a layer of leggings underneath for warmth, or her dirty boots that were now smearing a bit of mud on the nice truck interior.

That's when she really looked at the Mills family. Charlie was wearing the shiniest pair of loafers Lyla had ever seen. His button-up shirt's collar peeked over the opening of his sweater, and his hair was combed nicely to one side. If Charlie's attire wasn't weird enough, Sandy's hair was straightened and flipped out at the bottom. Her collared dress was yellow and white and buttoned in the front. Lyla could imagine her red heels on her feet if she could see them from where she sat. The father, whom Sandy introduced as Jim Mills, wasn't any different. They all appeared to match their 1965 crew cab truck as if they drove right out of a car catalog.

"Wow," Lyla couldn't help her curiosity. "Are you guys on your way to a car show or something? If so, you really hit the look."

Sandy and Jim glanced at each other with a stare that Lyla couldn't place. How long was it to the gas station again?

"So, do you walk this road a lot?" the man asked, ignoring her question. Something dipped in Lyla's stomach. It was happening again, a weird hitchhiking experience. She just needed to get to the gas station. They should be there soon, right?

"Only when I need to." Lyla was proud of her response. It didn't give away her schedule or indicate she'd be somewhere they could find her again.

"And today you needed to?" Sandy asked.

"Yeah," Lyla swallowed and peeked out the window. It was still dark out and foggy. Even with the headlights on, it was hard to tell where they were. Strange. She thought she knew every inch of Fire Trail Road.

"And how often do you need to, Lyla?" Jim asked. Lyla's eyes shot to the man driving the car. She racked her mind for a memory that wasn't there. She'd never told them her name.

"What's with all the questions?" Lyla gripped the handle on the truck door. "How did you know my name?"

"Hey, hey, it's ok," Jim said.

"Yes, I promise you we mean you no harm."

"Mom, she's getting the seat wet!" Charlie complained next to him. For a moment, Lyla almost growled at the kid. He'd dampen the seat, too, if he'd been out walking in the rain.

"I think you should let me out," Lyla said. "I can walk the rest from here."

"Oh, I wish you wouldn't leave." Jim frowned. His hands gripped the steering wheel until Lyla could see the bones through his knuckles. "We don't get to talk to people like you often."

"He's right, Lyla, we take this road all the time and never get hitchhikers. It's pretty exciting." Sandy's voice was sweet and pleading, and it made Lyla both want to stay and run at the same time.

"Nah, I think I'll pass." She hated being rude, but safety was her priority. "Just pull over here."

Jim and Sandy shared another look, and it made Lyla worried she'd have to launch herself out of the truck.

"We have to, Jim," Sandy said with reluctance. "It's time she knows the truth."

"The truth?" Lyla stuttered out.

The headlights of the truck flashed once, then twice. Lyla blinked to adjust her eyes to the dark again. When they did, it was the reflection of Sandy's face in the windshield that she saw first.

Sandy's face—her skin pulled back, as if sliced off. Her eyes were empty and lifeless, her neck and dress covered in shards of glass and blood.

"Let me out!" Lyla screamed. She couldn't keep the panic from tearing through her mouth. Unconsciously, she'd been pulling at the truck door handle. It was locked. But these old truck locks just needed to be plucked up. If she tugged it, the lock would release, and she could leave. She could tuck her head in and roll if necessary. She could—

"It's alright, Lyla!" Jim waved his hand back to calm her. His reflection in the driver's window was an image of his head halfway decapitated and leaning to the left. "I'm pulling over. I promise."

The truck slowed, and part of Lyla was both relieved and distrustful of Jim's intention to really let her go.

The lock was up now. She must have pulled it up with her shaking hands earlier. Lyla opened her door before the truck came to a full stop, and just as she slipped out of the seat, Charlie turned his face towards her to wave goodbye. It was smashed. Half his face was crushed, and his eyeball impaled on a small branch.

The truck door slammed shut with a whoosh of air before the engine revived. It sped off into nothingness, into the air of the early morning fog, as if it were fog itself. The chill of the wind cut through her clothes. Her body shook and shuddered from more than just the cold. She tried to take one breath at a time. In and out, she pressed her hand to her chest. She'd never believed in ghosts. She'd never believed in the tales of hauntings, but now, how could she refute the evidence?

On wobbly feet, Lyla turned towards work. Towards the gas station, she would need to walk the rest of the way to safety, light, and comfort. The fog was dense, though, and within a few yards her shoe hit something with a metal clank.

At her feet was a metal guard railing like the one from the bridge. It was on the asphalt, crushed and broken. Someone had hit it again. She patted her pockets for her phone. They were empty. Did she leave her phone in the ghost truck?

The fog rolled away, and Lyla could see it. The vehicle was flipped into the ditch.

The silver SUV. She was in no condition to call for help, even if she did have her phone. But she could at least check on the driver.

As Lyla approached the accident, she noticed a person standing on the road at the scene.

She sighed a shaky breath, grateful that someone else was already helping. Maybe they called 911? Maybe she could just pass the accident and go to work. Maybe she'd be in the way.

As Lyla got closer, her shoes became heavier, as if they were full of water. It had stopped raining, but the water was slowly climbing up her jeans. Did she step in a puddle?

"Hey, is everything okay?" Lyla called out to the woman at

the accident, but it was as if she didn't hear her. The woman was familiar in a way Lyla couldn't place. Like she'd been here.

Like this car had been here. Like she . . .

The woman. The one standing by the ditch.

Lyla's pants were soaking now. The water climbed up her shirt. The woman . . . she could see her closer. Her massive coat. Her gloved hands. It was—her.

Everything was wet. Her coat, her gloves, the ends of her hair. Wet coldness was crawling up her neck as she reached out to the mirror of herself from those months ago—herself staring at an accident in a ditch.

Then a car pulled over, and a man rushed out. The man who called in the accident was because Lyla had been of no help. Because Lyla couldn't move back then. He ran towards the SUV. He ran right through her.

She tried to yell, but she couldn't breathe. Everything came out as garbled water. It poured from her lips as she tried to scream. Tried to stop it. Tried to do anything.

"I told you she'd see the truth." It was Sandy's voice next to her. From her side, Lyla saw the ghost truck, the 1965 crew cab truck, slowly roll up next to her.

"She does every time," Jim remarked with a frown.

"Maybe this one will stick," Sandy said. "Darling, please get back in."

"She'll make the seat wet, Mom!" Charlie argued from the back.

"That's okay. We all make messes." Jim smiled at her. "Come on, ride with us. We understand better than all the others."

The others.

The accident started to fade away. Her lungs filled with air again. She was drying out, her hair and clothes as if they were all going backwards, as if they were all reversed.

The other drivers. The ones who'd told her to get out or given her weird looks. They were the living. The others.

Lyla weighed her options. The truth. The Mills. The comfortable and warm 1965 truck.

The road. The fog. And the insistent shiver she couldn't get out of her bones.

Then she reached for the door handle and climbed inside the truck's cab.

WENDIGO

JENSEN REED, MN.

Night-time insects drowned out the crunch of gravel beneath my shoes as my dog and I approached our street. It lay nestled on the edge of a suburb, more wilderness than the city, really.

Over a dozen houses lined either side, but only the center was lit by a singular streetlight. Some of the neighbors had little lamp posts in their yards, but they didn't give off a ton of light.

Decoy sniffed along the grass, tongue lolling from a long walk in the summertime heat. Unless the weather was awful, we did this nightly. A door closed as we turned onto the street, and I glanced towards Bernardo's light blue house. He stomped from the house to his garage in another bad mood. Definitely not my favorite neighbor, especially after he sent out letters asking to buy all of our houses and seemed offended when no one took him up on it.

We'd only gone a couple of feet when something crashed in his garage, followed by the clanging of metal and a strangled cry. Decoy and I froze. Before I could go see if the grumpy realtor was okay, Decoy let out a threatening growl, and his hackles rose. I slipped my hand under the strap-on his harness, not trusting a leash to restrain the large German Shepherd.

A cool breeze made my skin pebble, but I called, "Bernardo, are you okay?"

A thud against the garage door made me jump. Another growl emanated from my dog right before a figure exited, holding onto the doorframe for support. Even though he was hunched, I noticed how much taller he seemed than my neighbor. The desire to call out again dried in my throat as the stench of rot hit me. He stayed put, staring at the cement and breathing heavily. I gave Decoy a command to leave it, but I couldn't shake the feeling of a gaze on my back the entire way home.

A few days later, police lights lit my street while we readied for our walk. I noted the cars parked all around Bernardo's home, and instead of going that way, we crossed the street. I approached an older, single-story white house and knocked. It didn't take long before an elderly woman answered with a smile for me.

"Oh, Kaira, darling! What a surprise!"

She used one foot to keep her small dogs from escaping and stepped out to join me on the porch. I greeted her, then put my back to the drama unfolding behind me.

"Do you know what's going on, Mrs. Marr?"

Her pale eyes lit up in excitement. "Oh, I do! I heard whispers that Bernie has been missing for several days! His sister finally called the cops, and that's what they're doing. Looking for clues."

I tried not to smirk at the nickname I knew the man hated. "A few days?" I pet Decoy's head, but he was focused on the gap between Mrs. Marr's home and Ryan's house. If he had been home, I would have asked him first.

"Oh yes. She claimed he's been unresponsive since Sunday. So, about five days, that makes it.

No one has brought out a body bag, though. Maybe he ran off?"

"Anything is possible, I suppose." I felt Decoy tense against my leg and looked up just in time to see something dash behind the house. "Have you been okay, ma'am?"

"Oh yes, dear. Would you like to have some tea?"

I brought my focus back. "I need to take Decoy on a walk, but maybe tomorrow?"

"Perfect! Have a good night, Kaira."

She gave me a tight, grandmotherly hug and slipped back into her home. Feeling uneasy, I walked across the grass and peered into her backyard. Her garden was getting overgrown and looked thirsty, but nothing caught my eye. The tree line fifty or so feet from the house seemed calm, but I could feel . . . something. None of the neighbors on this side of the street were out, so we turned away, but the sudden silence left my heart pounding. Bugs and birds going silent was never a good sign. We did a quick walk, but the police were still there when we returned.

Only a day later, I mentally cursed myself for late-night research into local legends and folklore as I ran across the street, fear making my hands shake. I don't know what made me look out the window, but I'd seen Mrs. Marr ambling around to the back of her house after checking her mail, and then something grabbed her from the backyard, yanking her into the darkness and out of sight. I didn't even think of grabbing my phone. I just ran.

Ryan's lights were on, telling me he was home, but I went to her house first. Without lights spilling out from the house, her garden was eerily dark. I'd almost reached the motion light mounted to the back of her garage when the distinct crack of bone froze me in place. I knew it was in the mid-nineties out, but chills wracked my body.

A chunk of the fence was broken, smashed inwards, and a line of the carefully tended plants lay wrecked in a path to a hunched form in the center. Sensing me, the figure whipped around. My sudden backpedaling triggered the light.

Crouched on the balls of its claw-tipped feet with Mrs. Marr's bloodied body draped across its knees, the creature stared at me through sunken eyes on a skeletal face. Desecrated skin pulled so taut across its frame that parts of it had torn where bones protruded. The face seemed deer-like with its angular shape, but the teeth it bared at me through tattered, chewed-up lips were very humanoid. Mangy patches of fur covered spots of its body, but it remained mostly skin.

Mrs. Marr reached a shaking hand towards me, and my eyes widened in shock that she was alive with a hole in her chest. The creature covered her face with one hand, and long, talon-like claws effortlessly sank into her head, stilling her. My gaze jumped back to the creature when it cocked its head to the side and in an almost-perfect imitation of the elderly woman's voice called, "Kaira, dear?"

I could hear Decoy losing his shit at home and I knew if I didn't leave now, I wouldn't. It tensed, but I didn't stay to see why. I sprinted for my house, tripping over the curb and barely remaining on my feet. I slammed myself into the door, shoving it open just enough to get in before shutting and locking it. Decoy stood at the window on his hind legs, his entire body trembling in times with warning growls. I sank to my ass against the door, ignoring the alerts from my watch about too high of a heart rate, and tried to breath. I needed to call 911. What would I even say, though?

"Hi, this is Kaira Leigh, and my neighbor was just eaten by a wendigo."

OR . . .

I was being hunted.

My German Shepherd, Decoy, and I had been on our nightly walk, skirting along the edge of our neighborhood, which bordered a heavily wooded area in the suburbs of Minneapolis, when everything had fallen silent. Birds, squirrels, and even buzzing summertime insects fell quiet in the presence of whatever was watching me.

I kept walking but tried to follow Decoy's gaze to see what he'd noticed. All I saw were rapidly darkening trees from the setting sun, and our street's singular light was too far away for comfort. If it had been a one-off occurrence, I would attribute it to a human (me) startling the wildlife. But this was the fourth night in the last week.

"Leave it," I ordered, and he turned away from the trees, but his hackles stayed raised. We walked a little faster until the singular streetlamp that lit the middle of our street bathed us in light. I hurriedly unlocked the front door to our house, and we hurried in. Decoy went to his water bowl, and I paused in the entryway to kick off my sneakers. I yelped embarrassingly loudly when my phone rang. Fumbling to answer it, I tried to hide the waver in my voice.

"Hey, Mrs. Marr. Is everything okay?"

I could hear the smile in my elderly neighbor's voice. "Is everythin' okay with you, Kaira dear? You and that dog were sure movin' quick!"

I leaned back against the front door. Of course, she was watching. "Yes, we were just eager to get home and have ice cream. Would you like to join us?"

"Oh no, it's much too late for that. I just wanted to make sure you were okay."

"I appreciate it, Mrs. Marr. Have a good night, okay?"

"You first!"

I shook my head and went to shower, trying to shake the uneasy feeling that trailed me up the stairs.

Less than an hour later, as I sat with Decoy on the couch and enjoyed ice cream, I heard a soft knock on my door. Glancing at the time, I frowned and set my bowl down to check. The porch light was out again, and I couldn't see anyone. I'd just opened the door when Mrs. Marr called out.

"Kaira, dear?"

I froze. It sounded like her, but somehow wrong. Drawn out and . . . hollow. Goosebumps raced across my arms.

"Yes?"

"Kaira?"

I shut the door.

THE ARCHBALD POTHOLE

CORY LANIEWSKI, PA.

"I can't give ya everything, Eric, 'cause I don't really have everything," the old desk clerk said while he affixed his glasses upon his bulbous nose.

He reached into a drawer and passed by dozens of folders. They were all shoved to the front as the elderly man, presumably in his seventies, searched for something in particular.

"Anything you've got would be a huge help," the young reporter said in an unsure tone.

It was only a minute of his silence before the old man let out a soft sigh.

"And there it is," Mr. Kasprzak said slowly. He set the wrinkled folder down in front of the reporter, adjusting it slightly to be more centered on his desk. "I hope ya find what you're lookin' for."

"And this is everything, Mr. Kasprzak?" Eric asked.

"Sure is. Everything dat survived this long was kept inside this folder." The two men became silent as the reporter skimmed through the small number of loose-leaf papers inside the folder. The majority of the information was the general history of his destination: the Archbald Pothole and its state park.

As Eric looked over the documentation, he asked, "Now, uh, when you say survived, what do you mean by that? Did something happen to the files?" He pulled out his notepad and readied himself to jot more information down.

Mr. Kasprzak drew out another folder from the drawer he had rummaged through. This one bulged from a newspaper contained within it. He cleared his throat and pulled out the paper. As he folded back two pages, he said, "Have a look and you'll get da picture of why none of this nonsense ever made it outta da valley."

The reporter took the paper from the old man's hands and read over everything, though there wasn't much. The small article only took up half of the page, with two photographs of the pothole and the old Catlin House covering most of the designated section. He noted the highlighted portions and glossed over each of the lines twice. What information the reporter read was unclear.

He gathered that during the flooding of 1972 spurred on by Hurricane Agnes, the state experienced significant damages, with the capital city of Harrisburg receiving the worst of it. Businesses and homes were hit across the eastern seaboard, and the cleanup took years to fully recover from.

Lacking clarity, Eric questioned the old clerk. "What, exactly, does this flood have to do with the lack of articles on the Archbald Ghoul?"

"They were lost in dat flood," Mr. Kasprzak responded.

"Lost? You mean something happened to them?"

"Any file or newspaper article pertaining to da creature you're lookin' for was lost while en route here, to da Catlin House, for archiving. No other physical copies turned up outside of those few clippings, and nobody has had a story about it since."

Eric gathered up everything he had been given by the man and asked, "Do you believe that the story could be real? I mean, that's the whole reason I drove out here in the first place."

The old man's smirk was evident. He took a sip from his mug and wiped away the few drops of liquid that clung to his mustache.

"I believe some folks saw something out there. Probably just a vandal or a couple havin' relations. Nobody could ever make out anything 'cause of how dark it was during each sighting, but da monster got its start all da same. Now, if you can prove any of dat, like you're sayin'—"

"Oh, I think I can dig something up."

"Den you go get yourself a monster, son."

Eric lifted up the newspaper and a collection of files and asked, "Would it be alright if I made copies of these?"

The old man motioned with his head toward the doorway. "You'll find a printer just outside of da office. Ya passed it on da way in, just to your right."

Eric stepped into the hallway and copied each of the documents, skimming them as he went. After they were neatly tucked back inside their beige envelopes, he returned to the office and placed the original documents on the desk.

"One last thing, what's the best way to get there? I want to make it before sundown."

"You wanna go there tonight?"

"Sure do," the reporter said.

"A'right. From here, you're gonna wanna head back toward Mulberry Street, so just take a right when ya leave here, den a left, den another right. When ya get to Mulberry, hang a left and just keep goin'."

"That's it?" he asked sarcastically.

"Well, you're gonna get onto six and eleven, dat'll become the Scranton Carbondale Highway, and dat baby will take ya straight up da Eynon and da park will be on your right, just passed da first row of cars. If ya hit da legion of trucks, den ya gone too far."

The reporter adjusted his satchel's strap and nodded.

Well, that was somehow vague and straightforward at the same time.

"Thanks for the directions. Better be on my way."

As Eric was leaving the cramped office, the clerk yelled out, "Up da Eynon! Don't forget to just keep goin'."

"Right. The Eynon. Okay."

In the car just outside of the Lackawanna Historical Society building, the reporter's field aide waited. He had been going over research to pass the time until Eric returned. A muggy, mid-Autumn breeze shifted what was supposed to be a calm but humid day into a field journalist's headache. The rain that caught Eric entering the Catlin House had reduced to a drizzle as he left it. Steam rose up from the ground along the roads.

"For a society that's supposed to keep important documents, you would think they'd have had better systems, even back in the seventies," Eric spoke aloud as he sat in the driver's seat. The door shut with a thud as he continued. "This is it. No other documents or sightings, and not a single digital file."

Eric dropped the copied files onto Sully's lap as the van started up.

"Well, we are going to change that today! I'll get this stuff typed up and looking nice, backed up twice, and set it to send to Katherine first thing in the morning."

"It's still weird to me that no one has updated this information. No one has even reported a single sighting since 1969. Why wouldn't you want local folklore archived?"

While flipping through the documents, Sully commented, "It is possible it's just that good at hiding, or maybe it became roadkill and nobody batted an eye. Oh, or maybe it just vanished! Thing could be anywhere. That's an interesting angle."

"Let's keep it in the factual, alright? History and the now."

The van shifted into gear and began rolling away from the historical society's Catlin House. Its red brick and yellow-painted exterior crept back onto the University's property, on which it rested. Soon, the two men were on the main streets and headed for their destination. The sun fell to just above the hills of the valley and began to fill the sky with orange and yellow hues contrasting the purple-tinted storm clouds that remained over the city of Scranton, Pennsylvania.

Cars weaving back and forth through both lanes made for a tense but quicker driving experience. The reporters' GPS slated their journey at twenty-one minutes, but they arrived in just under eighteen. The van pulled into the parking lot around six-thirty. Sully took photos of the entrance as they passed by the wooden beams that served as gates whenever the park closed. No vehicles drove in behind them, so the men took the opportunity to capture the winding path that led into the park.

Two sedans and a truck were scattered around the parking lot, each with several spaces between, though no occupants were visible.

"The state page said the hours of operation were dawn until dusk and . . . the weather station says that gives us about two hours before it gets dark. But what's dark, really?"

"We've been out after dark before and did just fine," Eric said. "There should be more than enough light to set everything up and capture what we need to."

The two men stepped out of the vehicle, slid open the van's side door, and began unloading their equipment. Multiple small hard-cover cases rested beside the front tires alongside two camera stands. The men heaved duffle bags onto their shoulders and ran through a brief checklist.

With equipment in hand, they made for their first stop within the state park. It wasn't more than twenty yards from their vehicle that they set everything down onto the damp grass. Sully pulled out the copied documents and began reiterating everything they already knew.

"Okay, so dum da dum. . . uh, the pothole was made somewhere around eleven thousand to thirty thousand years ago. Pretty unspecific. The glacial waters dug it out . . . and it was stumbled upon back in 1884, six years after the founding of Lackawanna County. Okay . . ."

"Discovered by Patrick Mahon while mining for coal," Eric commented while snapping photos of the landscape. "That's the next line down. Just saying."

"Correct! Ding, ding, ding! Tell him what he's won, Johnny!" Sully set the documents inside an open case and glanced at the top page while pulling out a tripod.

Eric continued. "In 1914, the land on which the pothole resided was donated by the widow, Mrs. Hackley, to the Lackawanna Historical Society. The society gained one hundred and fifty acres by 1940, deeded the land to the Commonwealth of Pennsylvania, and then in 1964, the land was officially designated as The Archbald Pothole State Park."

Sully paused from his assembly of a mounted camera and looked toward his partner. "You really do have a good memory, don't you?"

"I just retain a lot," Eric said.

"No, buddy. That's pretty impressive for only glancing at the stuff. I definitely need some good shots to keep you from becoming a museum curator in Boston."

The two shared a laugh before Eric went his own way toward the pothole itself.

In his head, he added to the history.

In 1885, one year to the date of the pothole's discovery, sightings began of the alleged Archbald Ghoul. Twenty in total, ranging from coal miners to children, all after dark and within the state park, not isolated to the pothole itself. Then, in 1972, the floods eliminated nearly all records of the creature. Nobody bats an eye at their local history being erased.

Details are hazy: dark fur or scales, beady red eyes or none at all, claws or webbed feet. All we've got is that something lurked around this area for nearly one hundred years, then vanished.

Story of the end of my career . . .

He ascended the concrete stairs and strode across the extended slab walkway that jutted over the hole. He leaned over the sturdy metal railing and took several photos. Little light made its way into the pothole at this point in the evening, and Eric wished for fewer clouds to aid his exposure.

Always tomorrow, he thought.

The thirty-eight-foot drop was obscured by the hunks of rock that emanated from every side, almost like stairs descending into the semi-unknown. They knew how deep the hole went and generally what created it, but it still held a mystery. No photos of the bottom from within the pothole ever surfaced. Although aboveground shots told most of the story, there were nooks that were hidden from view, and cracks that attempted to shield their depth from sight.

The erosion of the stone's surface was smooth rather than jagged due to the waters that used to flow through it. Even the chips taken out of the walls were rounded off. From the depths, it almost appeared safe to hop deeper and deeper into the pothole, though the fencing around the site made it clear that trespassing wasn't allowed.

The flimsy wire and metal bars attempted to keep vandals from accessing the pothole, yet litter, bags of garbage, and graffiti dotted the underground landscape. A lone tree rested at the base of the hole, fallen and petrified. Safety trumped the thrill of diving into the pothole; Eric stuck behind the fence and took another photo.

Quick bursts of warm wind throughout the small clearing brought up the scents from damp stone and decaying leaves, which covered the flooring of the pothole. The perfumed air was calm between these gusts.

After several shots from various angles, Eric rejoined Sully in his movement of the equipment to their next location, leaving the setup camera focused on the stone walkway. They placed two other cameras: one that clung to the exterior of the fencing and looked down into the pothole, and one on a nearby tree roughly ten feet up after scaling a low-lying branch. Eric waited for his partner to ready his handheld camera before they began their segment, which ran them closer to dusk.

Eric recorded several audio notes as he walked around the pothole, and documented everything that he could see while Sully silently filmed the entire process. With only a single take completed before hikers emerged from the nearby trail, they decided to wrap up for the day and avoid the cuts they knew they would have to make around the pedestrians. They gathered their general equipment and made for their van as the other visitors of the park approached their own vehicles.

The two men allowed the cameras to record the hour and a half of decent lighting they had before removing the two tripod cameras and the fence camera. As if on cue, the park had one final visitor roll into the parking lot and exit their vehicle. A local officer checked that the park was empty from this entrance and hurried the reporters along with their removal of gear, though Sully was already waiting in the van.

The main roadway experienced an influx of cars travelling in both directions and held up their exit. They waited to turn in the direction of their hotel but remained just outside of the park's entrance as the officer pulled up alongside their van. He stepped out and pulled the park's gate across the entryway several feet behind their vehicle. At the first opportunity, the van merged into the expansive line of cars and made headway back toward Scranton . . .

Upon arriving at the hotel, Eric and Sully found a vacant table in the far corner of the lobby. They rested their bags down in what they hoped would be a quiet area to work for the time being. The hotel would be their home office for their stay, and they wanted to make the most of it. Sully began cycling through photos and videos while Eric mapped out where they would begin the following morning and the last day of their hunt.

Roughly an hour into their work, Sully's watch let off a soft chime, which prompted his attention.

"Weather update." He clicked his tongue while he scrolled through the tiny screen. "Looks like we have a twenty-six percent chance of seeing rain tomorrow."

"I like those odds," Eric said, eyes focused on his work.

"Yeah, not really a concern with the tree coverage. Should be pretty . . ." Sully trailed off.

Eric's head was facing the documents upon the table when he commented, "Pretty, huh? I'll make sure to take some photos of the flowers and little critters." With no response, Eric continued without looking up, "Not your style? How about the rocks?"

Sully remained quiet as Eric flipped over a map.

"Joking aside, we should capture some of the foliage.

Maybe make for some good background shots. Chime in whenever you want, Sully."

The table remained silent. Eric lifted his head to see his partner's attention fixed on one of the cameras. Sully's eyes darted back and forth while his fingers bounced around the camera's buttons. He leaned in and brought the display closer to his face as he studied the device.

Eric stood up and approached his partner's side of the table. He glanced over what Sully had sprawled out in front of him, but nothing of any real importance stood out. Eric leaned over the back of the chair his partner sat in and tried to get a good look at what was on the small camera screen.

The image was a still shot from one of their tripod setups. Its wide-angle focused on the pothole from a distance and gave an encompassing view of the landmark, including the slab of concrete that stretched over the gap, and an expansive shot of the park behind it. The walkway was what Sully zoomed in on as Eric walked up.

"I couldn't get it from any other frame, and I think this is the clearest image. This was from right after you walked away from the platform. What do you see?"

He handed the device to Eric, who briefly looked over the screen before handing it back to Sully. "I see . . . the pothole. Good angle, I suppose."

Sully shifted the camera so he could see the image too, then tapped on the center of the screen with the eraser of a pencil. "Right there! Tell me you don't see that?"

Eric had glanced around the room. He saw several people chatting amongst themselves at various tables across the lobby, along with a couple checking in at the front desk.

"See what?" Eric responded.

Sully circled the underside of the concrete slab with the eraser and said, "Right there! That's a hand!"

"A hand? I see a squirrel foraging for the moss on the underside of a damp stone."

Sully pulled the camera close to his face once again and asked, "You seriously don't think that that could be the creature?"

Eric made his way around the oval table and back to his seat. The voices of others mingled in the background, but he knew that their particular conversation, mainly due to Sully, had been a bit loud. Eric waved to his partner, then hovered his hand over the table's surface, suggesting they lower the volume of their conversation.

"I think . . . we will be there tomorrow with all the same equipment and can check everything out then."

Sully's expression shifted and was immediately followed by a preemptive retort from Eric.

"If we jump to anything, I would rather have more solid evidence that this thing exists beyond an out-of-focus frame in a video. That's all I am saying."

"I know . . ."

"Can't go jumping the shark."

"I got it." Sully lowered his head and looked over the table, then at the bags to his left and right.

"The trail cam. We left the trail cam strapped to that tree. It just might pick something up!"

Eric nodded.

"But that thing only had six hours' charge on it," Sully noted. "Think we can go back and snag it before it dies? I don't want to fall behind in our research."

"We are not going back to that park until it opens in the morning. You saw that it was locked up by the locals. What if they actually patrol that place, huh? Reports of trespassing and lewd activities after dark are jotted down in our notes. I don't want to get mixed up in that and have our equipment confiscated, even in the short term. That would put us behind."

"And that is why we go back tonight! In quick and duck out. You pull up to the gate, I'll jump out and head for the camera. You can drive by back and forth until you spot me—"

"Are you serious right now?" Eric asked.

"Yes! It wasn't even set in the all-weather box, just strapped to a tree. If it actually rains out there, that thing could get screwed up and we're down a camera."

"We can get it tomorrow. Besides, it's already dark out."

"Easier to get in."

"You're all set on this idea, aren't you?"

"One hundred percent."

The two men bickered quietly for several minutes before the decision was ultimately made to return for the camera that night. Eric dragged his feet, but Sully packed up their bags with haste and a smile on his face.

"And if the stories are to be believed, that the Archbald Ghoul actually exists," Sully said. "Then, now is the perfect time to capture it on film. Each eyewitness claimed to have had a run-in with the beast at night, after all."

Eric kept quiet while the van was loaded. Their drive from Pittsburgh took them just over five hours with traffic, and their hunt for promised documentation became several wasted hours on top of travel. Each library was either a dead-end or gave nothing more than what public domain searches provided. All they had were several scraps of newspaper articles and a few stories from the Historical Society. Eric wanted to call it a night and rest at the table before collapsing into a questionably cleaned mattress. However, he found himself behind the wheel one last time that evening in a return to his field work.

The drive back to The Archbald Pothole State Park was

quick. There were fewer cars on the road, though traffic buildup still persisted due to distracted drivers. A sense of commotion came from flashing red and blue lights emanating from just outside of a flea market parking lot off to the right-hand side of the van. Drivers slowed their pace in both lanes to catch a glimpse of the incident.

"Rubberneckers," Sully commented. "Slowing down the road, and for what? It's one guy in a massive parking lot."

"Three police cars would be enough to want to slow down."

"To the speed limit, maybe. But we aren't even doing that! Sheesh. At least we know we won't be bothered by the cops."

Hopefully, Eric thought.

Sully already had his seatbelt off and tucked behind him when they arrived at the park's entrance. His fingers were ready on the door handle. He laughed to himself as the van halted. "In and out. We got this. Maybe I'll even get a photo of the Ghoul."

He gripped a small camera in his left hand and quickly popped the door of the van open. With a leap, he was on the ground. The door slammed behind him, and he passed by the gate into the park.

Eric was quick to pull around to make his stop appear less suspicious than it already did. Good thing nobody stops around here. At least they don't care what we're up to. Eric made his way back down the road and passed by the officers they had seen only four minutes ago. The van came to a slow stop as the light at the intersection changed to red. He, much like the earlier drivers, focused on the potential traffic infraction in the middle of the nearby parking lot. One of the officers made his way back into his squad car. His emergency lights turned off as he backed away from the incident and pulled toward the intersection where Eric was stopped.

"Can't spin around in there. Guess it'll be the Salvation Army down the road instead."

He made his way only a fifth of a mile along the road before he came to his chosen parking lot and turned around. Nearby, a doughnut shop alongside the road saw its last employee leave the lot at the same time Eric passed by. The employee sped past Eric to beat the last light before the state park, where the lanes merged into one.

With no one behind him, Eric slowed as he approached the entrance, but hurriedly switched his foot to the accelerator when he spotted the officer from the intersection now parked in front of the gate.

"Shit. Gonna have to make another pass."

The van quickly caught up to the other cars and continued up the road. As Eric crested the hill, he noticed rows of trucks, Jeeps, and SUVs lining the side of the road on a small incline. His mind shot back to what the desk clerk had mentioned about going too far and chuckled. *If ya hit da legion of trucks, den ya gone too far.*

"Okay then."

When he reached the entryway to the dealership's lot, Eric managed to turn around without getting caught in the approaching line of cars and headed back toward the park. This time, there was no one in front of the gate, officer or Sully. His partner was unseen and he hoped that it was because he took to hiding when the police car showed up. He rolled his window down as he advanced on the gate and yelled out.

"Hey, let's go!"

The wood's rustling reply would have hindered any sound made from within the tree line, especially from someone hiding farther back. Eric didn't like the idea, but he parked his van, switched off the lights, and quickly made for the gate, which was still firmly locked.

Okay, so the cop didn't go beyond here.

He strode around the wooden barricade and hurried down the path into the parking lot. The area was completely devoid of light, and Eric had to allow his eyes to adjust to the darkness he passed through. As he approached the pothole, his pace slowed as he watched for the curb and large cracks along the ground.

Happy there's a fence around it, he thought as he approached the thin divider.

"Sully! We need to leave! Come on!"

Small creatures around the edges of the parking lot and along the hiking trail scattered from his yelling. Eric's body tightened up, and his eyes scanned the area.

"Let's go!"

The area was undisturbed and appeared identical to their first trip. Eric began going through the motions of remembering where they had set up each camera. Since he had been the one to wander off and get photos from the concrete overhang, he couldn't picture exactly where everything had been.

Maybe I'll get an idea if I step back up there.

He made his way to the center of the stone slab and peered around the area. Various locations seemed right, but he couldn't pick out where the tree camera was placed.

"Damn it. Sully! We need to go, now! Where are you!"

The sound of scuttling caught Eric by surprise. His words hung in the air. In the midst of the echoes, he picked out the distinctive sound of something beneath him. Something clawed at the stone he currently stood upon. He shivered.

Eric took a step toward the ledge and peered down into the hole.

"Squirrels and nothing more. I saw squirrels," he whispered.

The lack of light, natural or otherwise, made it difficult to pick out anything, but Eric could make out the massive stair-like chunks of stone descending into the blackness. Thirty-eight feet faded beyond eyesight except for one minute detail: a blinking light. Nearly unseen, the tiny red light flashed intermittently and then faded away into its dark environment.

He fell.

Eric's mind raced with what could've happened. He was panicked and missed the obvious and substantial bend in the metal railing several feet to his right. The freshly disturbed leaves in the pit below would have added to his confusion if he picked up on it before the returning winds chaotically returned them to how they were roughly twenty minutes ago.

The reporter ran in the direction of his van while screaming for Sully in the hopes that he was still somewhere among the trees. The van's glovebox, center console, and seats were torn apart in a desperate search for either his or Sully's cell phone. Nothing turned up, and without wasting another second, Eric turned the van around and headed for the nearest open business. All were closing, but he managed to reach a group of employees chatting beside their vehicles.

In his haste, Eric sped into the parking lot beside the cars and watched as each of the teens jumped backward. He did his best to convey the urgency of his point and, to his surprise, was given one of the employees' phones. Eric hastily dialed the police and hoped they were still in the area.

Only seven minutes passed before the red and blue lights returned to the area, followed shortly by firetrucks and an ambulance. Eric met the cavalry by the gate, where a firefighter cut through the chain that secured the wooden beams. The vehicles rushed into the state park, illuminating the darkened forest as if a carnival were ramping up. They began their search.

Throughout the night, Eric was questioned while the pothole and park were swept over. Some posed that he vandalized the fencing around the concrete slab and dropped his camera into the pothole, then created an elaborate story to have it retrieved. Eric laughed at first, but soon he realized that he was a suspect.

He recognized the officer leading the questioning as the same man who escorted Sully and himself from the park earlier in the evening. He wondered if Sully had been noticed at all, considering he was already in their van when the officer showed up.

Come daybreak, Eric was left with only one answer and more questions than he could comprehend. The officials at the scene stated that the blinking light at the bottom of the pothole belonged to a small camera. It was void of footage and subsequently handed over to Eric when he identified it as part of his equipment. Beyond that, there were no traces of Sully having been in the park that night, and no mounted camera was located by the police.

On his drive back to Pittsburgh, Eric's mind remained on his partner . . . his partner who saw a hand beneath the stone walkway and disappeared in The Archbald Pothole State Park after dark.

THE LONE RANGER

ROBIN JEFFREY, WA.

ON THE THIRD NIGHT OF HIS RIDE FROM CHEYENNE to Ft. Laramie, Chris bedded down on the open plain. It was risky—no cover to speak of, but the body of his horse lay down across from him—but the way Chris figured it, any person willing to ride out in this frigid cold with mischief in his heart wouldn't be dissuaded by a few paltry trees or the crest of a hill.

His breath crystallized in billowing clouds in front of his face, melting into water vapor as it reached the edge of the meager fire he had constructed from brush and buffalo chips. Head tilted back, Chris leaned against his saddle and looked up into the cloudless night, fingers toying with the harmonica that sat nestled in his jacket pocket.

Jason's harmonica.

It wasn't much of an inheritance. But he hadn't expected much. He'd have traded the harmonica for his brother back in a heartbeat. If only so he could tell him what a fool he was.

Getting killed over ten dollars' worth of poker chips in a Cheyenne saloon—the waste of it galled. But Jason had always been the hotheaded one of the pair, and their mother had predicted long ago that the younger boy would meet an unpleasant end.

Their mother they'd buried together in Denver, some three years back. Jason, Chris buried alone—just him, a preacher, and a teary-eyed hostess from the saloon whose name he had never quite managed to get in attendance as dirt was filled in over the pinewood box.

A quarter of an hour of digging, and his brother was nothing more than a memory.

Didn't seem right.

Chris took a pull of whiskey from the steel flask sitting at his hip, not bothering to lift his head as he swallowed. Tears formed at the edges of his eyes, and, with no one around to see them, he let them roll down his cheeks freely. The ride from Cheyenne to Fort Laramie was long, and without Jason, it was lonely.

With the fire crackling a few feet away, Chris drew his brother's harmonica out and began to play. The reedy strains of music spiraled up and out into the ether, melancholic and full of longing, and soon he felt compelled to put the instrument to one side and lift his voice to join the sound. He sang:

"O bury me not on the lone prairie."
These words came low and mournfully
From the pallid lips of the youth who lay
On his dying bed at the close of day."

Pausing to play another few bars on the harmonica, he felt the pain in his chest begin to ease, even as he sang the sad words to the song he and many other cowpokes knew so well.

"He had wasted and pined 'til o'er his brow
Death's shades were slowly gathering now
He thought of home and loved ones nigh,
As the cowboys gathered to see him die."

Lifting the harmonica to his lips once more, he broke off

mid-note as a low, sonorous voice from behind him took up the next verse, singing beautifully:

"O bury me not on the lone prairie
Where coyotes howl and the wind blows free
In a narrow grave just six by three—
O bury me not on the lone prairie"

Chris spun around, his hand falling towards the iron on his hip, but stilled when he took in only the empty, swaying grass which surrounded him. A rustle to his left drew his eye, and he nearly drew his gun when a deer-colored jackrabbit hopped into the firelight. Five pounds, about the size of a small cat, there was nothing unusual about coming across such a creature on the prairie at night—excepting, of course, the pair of polished horns that brushed against its long ears.

A jackalope.

Chris stared at the animal. The Jackalope stared back, sitting up on their back haunches and twitching their nose at him. Chris, for lack of a better option, relaxed back against his saddle and gave what he hoped would be interpreted as a friendly nod.

"Evening," he said, his voice shakingly only slightly.

"Evening," responded the Jackalope, not in the deep, booming bass of a moment before but a sweet, feminine lilt.

"You . . ." Chris' eyes darted from side to side. He swallowed hard. "You have a beautiful voice, ma'am."

The lady Jackalope tilted her horns in Chris' direction, her eyes shiny and black in the flickering light of the weak fire. "Same to you, young man."

Chris' horse shifted where it stood, letting out a sharp, loud huff of warm air through its muzzle. The sudden sound in the pregnant stillness made Chris jump. He glanced from the horse back to the Jackalope, worried his jerkiness had startled her away. But she remained standing on her hind legs, observing him placidly.

Chris wet his cracked lips with the tip of his tongue, and the taste that lingered there reminded him of some of the tales he had heard about Jackalopes. Moving slowly, he reached for the empty tin camping cup lashed to his saddle. Freeing it with a few tugs, he poured what he hoped was a generous amount of amber liquor from his flask into the cup and, leaning forward, placed it on the ground between himself and the Jackalope. "Whiskey, ma'am?"

He noted that the animal waited until he had withdrawn fully, but after a beat, approached the tin cup without further hesitation, hopping across the ground on all fours. "Mighty kind."

Chris watched with rapt attention as the female Jackalope approached the cup and, after a moment of fumbling, actually managed to get their paws on either side of the tin vessel and lift it off the ground. Would she sip from it as genteel as any lady sipping tea? No—he was relieved when, much more like the animal he was beginning to doubt she was, the Jackalope stuck its full face in the cup and lapped at the whiskey with its tongue.

Every child in Wyoming had heard stories of Jackalopes, of the strange horned rabbits that flitted across the empty plains and mated in lightning storms. They were fast, faster than the wildest stallion, and their horns were sharp enough to gore predators and keep themselves safe from meddling humans. Some people said they lured children out onto the plains at night by mimicking the voices of their parents, and the children were never seen or heard from again, lost to the wilderness forever.

Jason loved those stories. A lump formed unbidden in Chris' throat at the thought, and he swallowed it down with a rough clearing of his throat. The Jackalope pulled back from the cup and, looking slightly embarrassed at the fervor with which she had imbibed, put down the tin mug as gingerly as she could. Sensing her discomfort, Chris looked away, even though the last thing he wanted to do was take his eyes off the creature. He doubted she was dangerous, but he'd heard stories of Jackalope tricks. Maybe this was one of them?

"Where did you learn to sing?" asked his strange, new companion, a lilt of genuine interest in her voice that struck Chris as almost eerily human.

Chris tried on a small smile and found that it didn't feel entirely false. He crossed his arms over his chest, his fur-lined coat the only thing between him and the cold night air.

"Where does anyone?" he responded at length, a sideways smile lengthening. "From the birds in the brush, the good Lord above, and at my momma's knee."

The Jackalope wiped a few stray droplets of whiskey off her whiskers as she sat back from the cup.

"Sad song." She looked up into Chris' face, and her head fell to one side. "Sad man?"

Normally, he would've bristled at such an inquiry - at the weakness it hinted at. But there seemed little point in pretense with this creature, and he simply nodded, wiping what was left of the tear drops off his cheeks. "Yes, ma'am. It's my brother, he's . . ." He struggled with the words, though death was not a stranger to him. In the end, he looked away from the creature's warm gaze and managed to choke out, "He's gone."

He looked up into the starry heavens and tried hard not to weep again. It wasn't seemly, a grown man crying like a child. But he blinked the tears out of his eyes in shock when he felt a warm pat against his thigh and looked down to see the Jacka-lope sitting beside him, her paws resting against his leg in a gesture of comfort. She looked up into his face, and while he found her furry visage impossible to read, she seemed to have no such trouble with him.

"I'm so sorry." The little paw rose and fell against his leg. The Jackalope nodded knowingly, her gaze drifting from his face up into the star-filled skies above them. "I haven't seen my Henry since the lightning storms last year."

The human name threw him. Chris looked down at her in frank confusion. "Henry?"

"My mate." The Jackalope sighed and settled down beside him with her paws tucked under her furry body for warmth. "I suspect the damn fool has gotten himself hung up over someone's mantlepiece. Never was the brightest flash in the cloud."

Chris winced at the thought of all the jackalope heads he had seen in bars and homesteads across the state. Back teeth grinding, he let out a soft sigh. "I never thought . . . my condolences, ma'am."

"It's the way of the world," said the Jackalope.

A hollow sentiment that rang empty in Chris' ears and chest. There was a resignation in the Jackalope's voice that he resented, though he couldn't say why. She stared into the low fire before them and was silent for a while. "Josephine, by the way."

Chris removed his hat, feeling foolish for doing so and equally foolish for not having done so earlier. "Chris, ma'am."

"I hope you don't mind me intruding on you, Chris," said Josephine, rolling her tiny shoulders back, muscular and lithe under her fur. "But I heard you singing, out here, all alone, and I thought . . ." Josephine sighed again, lowering her head to the ground. "Well, I thought to myself, 'that there is a soul that understands loneliness'."

Chris shook his head, frowning. "I don't really." His fingers pressed into the crown of his hat. "Haven't had much time to be alone. All these years, it's been me and Jason. Not that we were inseparable or anything. In fact, we were really not much alike at all."

Chris had frequently been left confused and annoyed by his brother's actions, truth be told. Jason had been an impetuous youth and grew up into a wild and wayward young man.

Where he got this streak of trouble, Chris never did know. Their parents were good folks, ranchers and god-fearing Christians, and had done their best to raise both boys to appreciate a day's hard work and a night's quiet rest.

But Jason had never been one for work or quiet. He was always in one scrape or another, it seemed. One that Chris would inevitably have to help get him out of. But get him out of it he did, and Jason was always grateful. Always ready to greet him with a smile.

He'd miss that smile more than he'd realized.

"But I suppose you always had each other, was that it?" prompted Josephine.

"We did," said Chris. "That's why my momma said the good Lord blessed her and my pa with two children. So one would never be without the other. Now, course . . ." He felt the prick of saltwater at the corner of his eyes and kicked his heels into the dirt, scrunching his eyes closed tight. "Damn it. Damn it. I should've taken better care of him. This is my fault."

Josephine sat up, her whole body twitching as she shook her head. "No. You can't blame yourself."

"Can't I?" His teeth ground against each other, and the taste was chalky in his mouth. "If I'd been a better brother, a better friend—"

"He wouldn't have died?" There was an edge of anger in the sweet, soft voice that stung.

Chris retracted from it, even as Josephine edged closer to him.

"No one profits by thoughts like that. You don't and can't know that, Chris."

The young cowboy forced himself to take a deep breath. He uncurled his fists. "No. No, I guess I really don't." He gave a tired snort. "Feel like I don't know anything anymore."

"Life is about the uncertainties. Death . . . the certainty." Josephine's cottontail twitched and wiggled. "But that's not so bad."

Chris glanced down at his strange trail companion, tilting his head to one side. "Isn't it?"

"Uncertainty means chances. Chances for joy. For love. For connection in unexpected places." Josephine straightened up, placing both of her front paws on his leg this time, and looked up into his face. "I know it's lonely now, but you won't be alone forever."

He wanted to believe the strange creature. He sought comfort in her words. They were the first words offered to him since the telegram that told him of Jason's passing had reached him, which didn't make him want to cry. But Chris couldn't understand, and in his lack of understanding, he couldn't ignore the undercurrent of suspicion, of mistrust in this lady Jackalope's intentions. He shifted forward, just slightly, just enough so that he was leaning over the creature and, with one hand by his hip, he queried coolly, "You're taking an awful risk, aren't you, ma'am?"

Josephine didn't move apart from blinking up at him several times in rapid succession.

Chris shook his head once, hand moving closer to the handle of his revolver. "I could've killed you. Still could." He let out a shallow breath. "A man can make good money selling a jackalope."

Josephine stayed still. Her narrow chest rose and fell several times before she answered.

"Yes. It's sad but true." He felt her weight shift in her feet and thought she was fixing to run. "But . . ."

Muscles tense, Chris watched his visitor closely. "But?"

Without further warning or hesitation, Josephine hoisted herself up onto Chris' leg's fully, forcing him to lean back lest he get clocked by her antlers.

"I'm lonely too," she admitted, curling up in his lap. "And you have a beautiful voice. Hard not to trust a voice like that." She nodded to the harmonica that sat abandoned at his side, careful to avoid hitting him. "How about another song, young man? One of your brother's favorites, perhaps?"

Chris let his hand drift from his gun to the ground and felt for the harmonica in the dust. "Do you know The Cowboy's Dream?"

"Of course I do," said Josephine.

And as Chris began to play, her deep bass voice rang out across the cold, hard plains.

Last night, as I lay on the prairie,
And looked at the stars in the sky,
I wondered if ever a cowboy
Would drift to that sweet by and by.

Roll on, roll on;
Roll on, little dogies, roll on, roll on,
Roll on, roll on;
Roll on, little dogies, roll on.

The road to that bright, happy region
Is a dim, narrow trail, so they say;
But the broad one that leads to perdition
Is posted and blazed all the way.

. . .

They say there will be a great round-up,
And cowboys, like dogies, will stand,
To be marked by the Riders of Judgment
Who are posted and know every brand.

I know there's many a stray cowboy
Who'll be lost at the great, final sale,
When he might have gone in the green pastures
Had he known of the dim, narrow trail.

I wonder if ever a cowboy
Stood ready for that Judgment Day,
And could say to the Boss of the Riders,
"I'm ready, come drive me away."

The tears flowed freely down Chris' face, but he felt his lips curling into a smile despite the sadness in his heart. He kept playing, loud and long, and Josephine kept singing, and in some small way, with the Jackalope on his lap and the song heading heavenward, Chris began to understand that as long as you kept an open mind and loving heart, a person would never be truly alone.

THE HANNAH HOUSE

BREANNA DAWN, IN.

I sit on the bricks at the most haunted location in Indiana. Chills run up my neck as a cold breeze brushes past my hair. I can feel the texture of the bricks under my fingertips, trying just to take in every part of this house. "Frozen in time, 1858 . . . I could only imagine how they must feel," I whisper.

The bricks are cold under my fingers as I slowly make my way to stand. I take a deep breath and walk to the front door with the equipment in my hand. "Let's do this," I breathe.

"Iris!" I turn to look, and one of the volunteers makes their way to chat. "I wanted to wish you luck on your investigation!" He smiles.

"Thank you, Trevor, I look forward to it," I smile and walk towards the stairs. The railing is wooden with deep browns and a beautiful rustic appearance. I gently place my hand on the railing and close my eyes as I take fifteen steps to the top.

As I reach the last stair, I open my eyes, making my way to the first door I see and turning the handle. I am met with an overwhelming scent that brings me back to a time when my grandmother was alive. I look around the room, and my eyes catch a photograph on the bedside table.

I note the appearance of a couple, they look so . . . unwell. The bedding is old, with floral printing and a ruffled bedding skirt. The headboard is wooden with an almost suffocating dark brown.

The smell of wood meets my nose, it's an earthy subtle must that clings to the memories of her well-loved bedframe. I am alone in this investigation but then again, I am not really alone when spirits are lingering around me.

"Bye, Iris, I am heading out now!" Trevor yells from the bottom of the stairs.

I told him thank you, and he shut the door behind him. The silence is deafening. I am okay with that. I begin to unzip my bags and take the cameras out to set up in the most important places of activity. One in the kitchen, living space, stairwell, bedroom halls, and the cellar. I walked to the kitchen, and there was a note on the counter:

Iris, I bought some beverages and food for your stay here this weekend. Talk to you on Monday!
-Trevor-

The hospitality was warm, and I couldn't help but giggle. I open the double doors to one of the fridges. That's right, two ginormous fridges! I assume for catering weddings and events. There was so much food! Jackpot! I grab some lunch meat, make myself a ham sandwich, and add some chips to the side. I set my plate down, debating on what drink to pick.

My eyes glaze over when I see Cherry Pepsi! Hunched over the counter, I look around and admire the beauty before me. "Your home is beautiful. I thank you for having me," I say casually in the air. I take the last bite of my sandwich and toss the paper plate in the trash. I decided to do a walk-through of my own before the initial nightly routine. Holding my Cherry Pepsi, I make my way to the front of the house. There is something about the floors creaking underneath me and the warmth of the colors around me. It sends me into the comfort of all things old and cherished.

There is always a sentimental ache when I see objects that were once loved and are now forgotten. I continue to make my way around the house, to be met back in the kitchen. I throw my Cherry Pepsi can into the trash and make my way back to my room.

It's 10:30 PM on a Friday, and I don't usually start my investigations until 3 AM . . .

Unless, of course, something wakes me in the dead of night. No pun intended. Which happens more than you think. I drag my suitcase across the floor and use my entire body strength to throw it onto the bed, eager to locate my sweater and leggings to change into. I throw my long brown hair into a ponytail and sit at the old desk chair. The smell of leather wafts over me. Glancing over all the cameras to ensure they work and doing a few odd and end things. I look at my phone's clock, which says 11 PM. I crawl into the old bed that creaks beneath me.

I pray before I close my eyes. "God, I pray that you guide me through this investigation and help me bring these people to the light to escape the nightmare they are reliving. They deserve freedom and your loving embrace. Help me find the words to set them free . . ." *Amen.* My eyes feel heavy, and sleep finds me.

I wake with a suffocating breath of something burning. The smell is traumatic and indescribable. I toss in bed, trying to recall the details I obtained before coming. The legend says

Alexander Hannah was a sympathetic man whose house was a haven for runaways along the Underground Railroad. Alexander would keep them in his cellar.

The library newspaper from the research section mentioned that an oil lamp was tipped over by accident, setting the space on fire, and those who were beneath the home, cramped in the cellar. There hasn't been any real proof of this, but that is why I am here. I am here to help guide them to the light, to set them free from the recurring nightmare. I ran to the table to check the cameras in each room. I look at each one slowly, and I don't see anything. Weird. I glance at the clock on the computer. It's 3 AM.

The door slowly opens with an eerie sound that follows, and I freeze. My breathing slows down, and the silence envelopes me. I can hear my heartbeat pounding in my ears. I walk slowly to the doorway and glance back at the camera footage. The camera misses this angle, so I am forced to move closer. There's a figure of a woman in a beautiful dress and a large hat. She walks past the door. I jump back and lose my footing. Luckily, I catch myself on the bed, collecting my emotions.

"Okay, Iris! You have done this a million times, you can do this, doofus," I chuckle. I won't lie, the fear inside me is like an exhilarating experience. It's not a high that I can get riding a roller coaster, but the end goal is even more satisfying, and that is to help them pass to the life of everlasting happiness. I walk to the door with my EVP box so I can hold conversations with them.

I neglect the cameras behind me and continue through, not knowing what will happen next. The smell intensifies as I make my way down the stairs. The woman I had seen earlier looks back towards me. I have a feeling she wants me to follow her. They always do. Slowly, I walk a few feet behind her. She is leading me to the cellar. My heart is pounding so hard that my chest is shaking.

The woman disappears outside the cellar door. The smell is potent, but my senses are acclimated to it. I walk through the threshold of the cellar. God has given me a gift to see the unseen for a reason. This is a passion that I take great pride in because I am doing the work God intended for me. I am saving the broken and saving them from the evil lurking within these walls.

My EVP box is going crazy, static is coming from the speaker, and I am trying to focus on a clear voice. "... fi ... fir . . . fire." The voices are muffled, but the sound of fire crackling plays in my mind, not understanding their pain, but I can feel it down here.

The cellar is dark and reeks of damp earth. I can feel the cold on my face. I try to locate a light, reaching my hands out, I feel for a switch, but only to feel an attempt of a hand wrapping around mine. I have enough experience to know that wasn't something, that was someone.

The meter goes silent, but the words hit me with heavy force: "Come with me." The voice was gentle but worried. I followed, frantic. I needed to keep up. We came to a stop, and I was unable to breathe. My words couldn't come out; the only thing that came out was tears. I could see them. I could see them in their misery and pain, huddled together in fear as if we were still living in 1858.

"Hello," I whisper. They all look up at me in silence. "I come to help you." I look around and find an old wooden chair in the corner. I grab it and sit down in the middle of the cellar. My head is down as I try to collect myself and wipe the tears from my cheeks. They don't need my tears. They have cried enough.

"Who are you?" A voice calls out.

I look up and straighten my posture. "My name is Iris, I am here to convince you to let me help set you free."

A woman and a man come forward. I have seen them before in the historic photographs of Hannah's House. It was Alexander Hannah and his wife, Elizabeth Jackson. They were crossing under the curved door frame, their eyes heavy, their faces long. I peer down at Alexander's hands, the same hands that built this twenty-four-room home. My heart aches.

Alexander digs his feet into the floor. I presume it was a habit when he was alive. "It was an accident, I was only trying to spare their lives and free them from those who were wicked," Alexander explained with his head down.

I can see the pain in his raspy, low voice. "Mr. Alexander, you are a man of sympathetic character, and I know you meant well for these people. You are, by God's grace, a man of good," I say, fighting tears.

A voice startles me, reaching over the hums of the others crowded about the cellar. "How are you going to help us, woman? We have been stuck here for people's amusement. We have tried to leave this house only to be brought back to it." It is then that I see a young man present himself to me with disgust.

"I know that you have been trapped here and endured the most painful memories that continue to recur from that very night," I closed my eyes and saw the word forgiveness. I have to deliver these messages that are coming to me.

Although I had to think before speaking.

There was a long pause between me and the people before me. "Mr. Alexander, do you feel guilty, like this was your fault?" I ask hesitantly in hopes he doesn't think I blame him.

"Mam, I couldn't continue seeing what was before me. I love everyone and have always been a loving person and caring to all. I wanted only to help and to save the lives I could. I left the lamp in the cellar to help guide their way through the tunnels. I will forever blame myself for us being trapped in this house," He finishes with a sniffle as his aiding wife holds onto him.

"Mr. Alexander, are you a man of faith?" I ask him.

"I feel my faith has diminished, young lady. Why must you ask?" He questioned with heartbreak.

"God wouldn't have led me to this mission if He felt it wasn't on the right path. He led me to you, to this house. He works in ways that we don't understand, and I feel that he was with you when you helped these people to safety. Your faith may have diminished, but God never walked away. You have to forgive yourself, Alexander."

It's silent at this moment, Alexander is sitting on the ground with his wife. I slouch in the chair due to exhaustion. Something told me to look up, I opened my heavy eyes.

The others walk into the underground tunnel and disappear. My jaw dropped, leaving me with Alexander. Just Alexander. I look around me to ensure that we really are here, just me and him. I find myself sliding off the chair to bring myself closer to him.

"Alexander, look around you," I said.

He finally breaks from the darkness and looks around him slowly. I have never seen every emotion displayed in the way he presented himself. "Where is everyone? Where is my wife?" he cries out.

I look at him, and my eyes meet his. "You know, I never used to believe in spirits or the nature of the afterlife. I lost someone dear to me, and it hurt every ounce of my being. She was my grandmother, a woman who was always spiritual with God. She would make every day bright just by the way she would present herself for him. The Bible was her diary, and her silent conversations with Him were special. The day my grand-mother passed, I was there with her.

"She was frail and quiet, not like she was when I was younger. She reached out for my hand and didn't let go. I felt her presence slowly fading, and she was gone. I felt her in a way that I have never experienced in my entire life. I still feel her with me, guiding me into every investigation. Then I started seeing spirits all around me asking for help! It was my will to get those who are forgotten and lost, and bring them to the light. Alexander, I am here to help you understand that sometimes letting go hurts, but if you don't let go . . . You're only going to be stuck in the same spot for the rest of your life," I express.

Alexander tries to put his hand on mine. The coldness sends a chill down my spine. I feel the sympathy from him and the brokenness he displays. "This moment I am sharing with you is a moment I feel we needed together. I want you to know just how amazing you are and how brave you were to care for the people who were in harm's way. I know it must have been scary to go against what was not accepted." I sniffle.

"It was extremely hard. It was forbidden if we hid them and aided them. God was indeed working through me during those times. Come with me." He says.

I come to a standing position and I walk alongside him. We are just outside the tunnel door. There is a barrel that once held the oil lamp. I look harder as the darkness makes it unbearably hard to make out objects. I noticed a Bible in pristine condition with absolutely no damage to it.

"Before the fire, I set the lamp on the barrel and a Bible so that the runaways could be in the presence of God. To learn his ways and to have faith. The night of the fire, I was returning home, and the flames grew bigger and bigger, smoke bellowing from under the door of the cellar. I burned my hand while turning the knob to save them, but when I went down there the flames were so big I struggled to save them. The fire pulled me into its vortex." He breathes.

"Alexander, YOU tried to save them! You sacrificed your life to save them! This was brave and heroic of you. He brought the runaways to the light and your wife. The opportunity was always there, but sometimes we are so blinded in the darkness that we don't know how to get to the light. Alexander, you need to find it within yourself to see that you are not to blame for the fire. The Bible withstood the fires, and Sir, if you have faith . . . even just a little bit of it, you will see that as a child of God, you are safe." I breathe.

I find myself locating somewhere to lean against as my body is aching and cold. I shiver through my teeth and close my eyes for just a moment.

Time went by, but it felt like hours.

"Iris, I-I- I am ready to go into the light. I am ready to let go." He pleads.

I look at him, mustering the courage to stand once more. "Go to the light, Alexander, you are free, and He will show you the way," I whisper, motioning with my hand in the direction. A light shining faintly into the tunnel that was once dark begins to grow stronger. I feel warmth on my face.

Alexander slowly walks into the tunnel and looks back at me. "Thank you," he quietly says. The warmth and light fade into the distance, and it is dark again.

I fall to the ground in exhaustion and curl up. I lay on the cold concrete floor, and my eyes started to feel heavy. I fell into a deep sleep. I woke up, still on the cold concrete floor in the cellar. I found the strength to get up. Moaning in pain to stretch my body, I slowly make it to the bedroom. Looking at my phone, I didn't realize it was Sunday afternoon!

"I slept that long?" I let out a belly laugh. I step into the bathroom and run the water. I dry off and make my way to get some clothes on.

"Well, I suppose I can call Trevor and tell him he can come now." I didn't want to wait to leave until Monday. My work here is officially done in the Hannah house.

My phone rings. "Hello?" Hey Trevor, I am calling because I finished my investigation and think I am good to head out of here." I say with a sprinkle of accomplishment in my voice.

"Hey Iris!! Yes, of course! I will head there now. It should only be about fifteen minutes. See you soon!"

The phone clicks on his end.

I gather my equipment and pack it up. I take my bags and bring them down by the front door. "Oh, I forgot something!" My phone is still in the room I stayed in. I run up the stairs and retrieve my phone. I also grabbed the Bible that was once in the cellar. I run back downstairs, and Trevor is already hauling my belongings to my car. I gave him the keys to the house before getting into my car.

"Thank you, Trevor! You outdid yourself on the Cherry Pepsi! Thank you, Oh! I also took some for the road," I smiled, what can I say . . . I am a sucker for Cherry Pepsi!

I take a look at the house, put my seatbelt on, and head down the road. Indiana sunsets really are breathtaking. My Cherry Pepsi in hand, and a little bit of Metallica playing in the background.

My phone rings through the radio. "Hello?" I ask almost like a question.

"Yo, Iris, it's Renee, you up for investigating Indiana Central State Hospital?" she asks. I look at my steering wheel and make a U-turn.

"Are you kidding? Already on my way." I shout. Looks like I am heading back into good ole' Indiana.

THE LIME KILN HAUNTING

LIZ SULLIVAN-FISK, WA.

The air felt damp and crisp as I stepped out of my car. It had just finished a fine drizzle not twenty minutes ago. The sun, tempted to peek out from the cloud cover, could just be glimpsed beyond the trees. Glancing around and taking in my surroundings, I went around to the back door of my old Jeep, grabbing my backpack for today's hike.

"A perfect October day for a nice hike," I muttered to myself. I hadn't planned on hiking today, but I knew I had been cooped up for far too long in my house with the walls pressing in and my mind needing settling. I had grabbed my pack that was always set with the basics, a couple of water bottles, my wallet, and keys, and had then found myself driving here, surrounded by greenery, at the trailhead of the Lime Kiln Trail. It wasn't far from home, at least.

I began walking to the path, passing the large signs containing some of the history of the trail. I'd read it many times. The old kiln was used to cook limestone mined from the area into lime, and the railroad tracks transported the lime to be smelted into ore. It was all abandoned in the 1930s. The only bits left today are the giant kiln and some other remnants of the past, such as bricks and some bits of saw blades and steel rail.

Damp ferns brush my jeans as I proceed to the trail itself, a sea of green before me. I feel like I am transported to a fantastical world every time I hit the trails, and this trail is no different. Moss drips from the tree branches, and the ground is covered with ferns and blackberry bushes, unfortunately, no longer in season. One foot in front of the other, I press forward into the forest.

As I progress further, I can hear ducks splashing in the nearby pond, though hidden from view by the vegetation. A little farther forward, I make my way down a slight hill, crossing the wooden bridge. Stepping carefully so as not to slip, I continue on. I can hear the creek that will soon join the river. I know it's not much farther until reaching the kiln. I'm already starting to see signs of it coming upon me. A couple of bricks here, a broken saw blade there.

Not much farther after, the giant kiln looms up to my right. Looking like something out of an ancient jungle, the kiln stood 20' high with moss covering the old bricks. A couple of broken saw blades lay to the side of the kiln. A slight path around the kiln was worn down from all the visitors to the area. I only stop to look briefly before continuing on.

"Not much farther till I loop back," I think to myself. The trail forks just ahead, where it loops by the river and the old bridge site. The bridge no longer stands, but you can still get down to the river near there on a nice day and chill on the riverbank.

I hadn't even made it two hundred feet when I felt a sudden chill over the course of my entire body. Every hair on the back of my neck prickled. I glanced around, trying to determine what may have sparked my senses. The sun was still shining through the trees, and I saw no one around.

Starting to think I was just mentally tired, I went to turn back to the trail. As I turned, just in my peripheral vision, I caught sight of something indistinct. I spun to get a better look, and it was gone. At this point, I felt my senses start tingling again. I decided to turn back and make the trek back to my car, far less casually than before.

It wasn't long until I had returned to the trailhead. Throwing my stuff in the back of my car, I slid into the driver's seat and sat there for a second. "What did I just see?" I whispered. I shivered at the thought of what I believed I saw, not wanting to believe it. A trick of the light, nothing more. After all, ghosts aren't real.

Over the course of the drive home, I worked hard to convince my traitorous brain that some drops of rain from earlier must have dripped from the leaves and caught the light of the sun just right. The cold feeling? Just a temperature change being so close to the water. I swung by one of the many coffee stands in town, grabbing my usual quad-shot mocha before continuing on home.

Pulling into my driveway, I could see my cat, Ollie, hanging out in his favorite window. A window where he could do as cats do, and judge everyone from afar. His favorite pastime. I grabbed my backpack from the back and proceeded into my house.

The following day, I had anything but forgotten my mysterious encounter on the trail. At work, I found myself continuing to think about it and continuing to fail to convince myself it was nothing but a trick of the light. "The sensation felt so real," I think. The abrupt cold, the senses tingling, seeing a misty flutter out of the corner of my eye. Even taking a long, hot shower when I got home hadn't helped alleviate the cold feeling that had lingered.

Just then, I found myself pulled from my thoughts when

my best friend, Kere, walked into the room in her usual jovial manner.

"Hey girl! Are you ready for the parade this weekend? I can't believe it's already this weekend and we have so much to do! Still need to create a banner and finish coloring the posters for the car door. Oh! Plus, making sure everyone has something they can wear! Oh hey, what did you do this weekend?" Kere exuberantly rambled.

It was in her nature, talk a mile a minute to the point one wondered how much caffeine was too much and if she had yet to pause for breath.

"Yeah, feeling mostly ready, I guess. Still a couple of things to add to my outfit. I have Maria working on the banner, I'm sure we can get some of the other kids to finish coloring the posters," I responded. "I went for a hike yesterday, just out to the Lime Kiln trail."

"Oh, how was it?" answered Kere.

"It was ok," I remarked. "The weather held out, and there weren't many people out."

"Well, that's good then! I'm glad you got out of your house for a bit, I know we have been pretty busy with prepping for the parade and trying to get all the kids ready," Kere said.

Busy was an understatement. Kere and I both worked for the local school. So not only were we busy preparing for the parade, we were also dealing with overly excited teenagers, some of whom were overly excited at being social again in the beginning of school rush. Everyone is swapping stories about their summer and what they did, sometimes barely being able to contain themselves to actually listen to the lesson.

As for the parade?

It wasn't just any parade. It was Railroad Days. A town tradition celebrating the town's history in railroads, and one of the biggest town events of the year. Every year, it was a whirlwind getting a float put together in time for the parade for all the kids. The kids always pulled it off though and oftentimes came away with one of the awards.

A good time all around.

"Hey Kere, about that hike I mentioned," I said.

"Yeah?" replied Kere.

"This is going to sound strange, but I saw something weird out there. Like a potentially supernatural type of weird," I whispered the last part. I still didn't want to admit it.

"Like a ghost? Or are we talking about some other kind of being? Did you see Bigfoot?" she exclaimed.

I rolled my eyes. Kere was obsessed with Bigfoot. "No, it wasn't Bigfoot. Of that I'm sure. It's just when I was out there, I had just passed the kiln when I suddenly got a severe chill, and not long after that, I had the strange sensation of something nearby. When I turned, I glimpsed something out of the corner of my eye, but when I looked, it was gone."

"Well, as disappointing as it is that it is not Bigfoot, I am curious as to what you saw," Kere replied. She got a look of concentration on her face before brightening again. She proclaimed, "We should go out together and see if you see it again! Let's go on Sunday to celebrate being done with the parade stuff!"

"You sure we will have energy for that?" I remark, raising my eyebrow. I know from years prior how much goes into parade day.

"Oh, come on, we aren't that old yet. Let's do it!" Kere declared.

"Eleven o'clock too early for you?" I shoot back.

"Nope, my kids will have me up at the crack of dawn. I swear they don't know the meaning of sleeping in," she grumbled.

I snort. "Okay, well, it's a date then. I need to find Maria to see if she needs help with the paper cutter for the banner. See you in a bit!"

I proceed on my way, turning my thoughts back to the upcoming parade and the rest of my day. The rest of the week progresses quickly. Railroad Days itself swarms up fast. Before I knew it, it was finished. The kids had worked hard, and they could proudly say they took home the "Best Float" award. They earned it for sure.

On Sunday morning, I spend some time just sitting on the couch while sipping my coffee out of my favorite mug. A "book-trovert," as the mug claims, if I didn't have somewhere to be in a few hours, it would mean I could be seen curled up on this very couch reading the next book on my to-be-read pile. I think a pirate novel is next on my list. Or perhaps something about mermaids. At any rate, I have a little over an hour before I need to meet Kere at the trailhead.

The day is cloudy, and rain is not far off, I'm sure. Typical for the Pacific Northwest, especially this time of year.

I unfold myself from the couch and rinse my dishes in the sink. Heading upstairs, I see Ollie perched on the shelf at the top of the stairs. Waiting for pets like usual. I stroke him and scratch his ear briefly before proceeding to get dressed for the day.

When I get to my car, I mentally double-check that I have everything I need. Wallet? Check. Water? Check. Raincoat? Check. I get settled in my car and pull out of the driveway.

Driving through town, I see little remnants of yesterday's festivities. It is rather quiet out. I guess everyone else is still recovering.

When I arrive at the trailhead, there are no other cars around. I shoot off a message to Kere about having arrived at the trail. Sitting back, I look at the green foliage ahead. There is some fall color starting to show mixed in with the eternal green.

My phone dings, a response from Kere. "Running five minutes late!"

No rush, I think to myself, *we have plenty of time to explore.*

A couple of minutes later, I hear the low hum of a vehicle, and I see Kere's blue Chevy truck pulling into the lot. I get out of my car as she finishes parking. A slight rain has started. I pull on my raincoat and slip on my backpack as she gets out of her truck.

"Hey! Sorry, Darrel didn't want to get dressed when I went to drop him off at my mom's house," Kere remarked.

"Don't even worry about it," I responded, "we have plenty of time today to see if we can find my possible ghost friend."

"How far is it until the kiln?" asked Kere.

"Not terribly far. Far enough, though, that I bet we will be damp with this rain." I quipped.

After Kere finished getting her gear situated, we set off into the trees. We walk in silence as the birds chirp above and around us. We tread carefully in spots as the recent rains and dirt have created a slippery mush of mud in some areas.

We make our way down the hill and across the bridge, occasionally remarking on the scenery. I point out the few bricks and such along the way as we draw closer to the kiln. A little way farther, we see the kiln loom up through the misty rain, looking greener than ever with the moss adorning it.

"So where was it that you saw your ghost?" asks Kere.

"It was just a little farther down, I had just walked past the kiln and didn't make it much farther before that cold chill hit me," I replied.

We continue closer to the spot where I had originally felt the sensation. I'm glancing left and right, trying to see if I see anything in my peripheral vision. Nothing. No flicker of something indistinct. No cold sensation. I glance at Kere and raise my brow.

"This is the right area, but I'm not seeing or feeling anything," I murmur.

"It could be that it was nothing then, or maybe you were just here at the right time to happen to see it." Kere asserted. "Maybe, if it was a ghost, the time you were here last held some significance to it, so it appeared."

"Maybe," I said. "At any rate, shall we continue the trail, or do you want to head back? The trail loops around a little way ahead."

"Let's finish the trail, and then we can go back and get dry," responded Kere.

We pressed forward and continued down the path. I can hear the river ahead, swirling a little stronger with the recent rain. The trail starts to curve as it goes to loop back to itself. We follow it quietly, listening to the river, and I wonder about my experience last weekend. Did I imagine it?

We are close to passing the kiln again as I continue to look around for any sign of my ghostly friend. Figment of my imagination is more like it. "It must have been the pace of life in recent weeks," I think to myself. I am pulled from my thoughts as Kere gasps.

Grasping my arm, Kere whispers, "Look! Just to the right of the kiln!"

My eyes dart to where she indicated. Sure enough, a little glimmer of shape is floating there. Not quite fully formed, more like an outline, a fuzzy outline. We crouch by the ferns beside us, not that they do anything besides share the moisture that coats them.

"What do you think it is?" I ask.

"I think you were right about it being a ghost. That is as ghost-like as I could imagine." Kere murmured.

I glance over at the kiln and notice the glimmer has taken on a more defined shape. It looks more person-shaped than before. I look at Kere and then back at the figure. It seems to just be waiting.

Hoping it wasn't about to be a "Ghostbusters" moment where I get slimed or something, I stand up and cautiously take a step forward. I hear Kere just beside me. The figure shimmers and looks like it may disappear. I stop, hoping it doesn't go away. The figure seems to have paused in its potential departure. I get the feeling it's regarding me with faint curiosity.

Its form is more solid in shape now, the gray sheen of smoke-like vapor being more defined. I can tell the figure appears to be a man. He looks like he is dressed in well-worn work clothes, but nothing that would have come out recently. Wearing trousers, a shirt, and a jacket, he looks like what I'd imagine someone from the early 1900s wearing. More precisely, he looks to be dressed as some of the men pictured in the historical photos were. I'd seen enough photos of those who had worked the area in the kiln's heyday. I slowly step a little closer. The man doesn't move. I am now near the sign that gives some insight into the kiln. I glance at Kere, unsure of what to do. How does one interact with a ghost?

"Were you a worker in the kiln?" I hear Kere ask.

The ghost nods.

I find myself asking, "Are you able to speak?"

He jerks his head to the side. I guess not then.

"Why are you here?" Kere prods. The ghost tilts his head at her, seemingly in thought. He then responds with what could best be described as a shrug.

"You don't know why?" I ask. Another jerk of the head.

"How did you die?" inquired Kere. He points at the kiln.

"So you died while working with the kiln?" she continued. A nod. I think back to some of the dangers of working with lime kilns. Falling in was a possibility. The other danger was the fumes from the lime burning. If the ghost was appearing as he was when he died, then I was sure it was a safe bet he hadn't burned in the kiln but had perhaps suffered the fumes too long. He looks at me and nods.

"Can you hear what I'm thinking?" A nod. Well, that's kind of cool, but also not. It's weird to think of someone being able to read my thoughts.

I look to Kere, who also looks a tad perturbed at the revelation. Just as I'm continuing to wonder about the idea of mind reading, I hear a slight crack nearby. Kere and I both turn to the sound, only to find another hiker making their way closer. When we turn back to the kiln, the ghost is gone. We glance at each other and silently agree we should start our trek back to the cars. The other hiker passes us, and we quietly make our way up the path. A little farther up, we feel the need to turn around to glance back at the kiln. The other hiker is now out of sight. Looking at the kiln, we see the shimmer has reappeared and appears to wave. We wave in return before resuming our walk.

The trek back to the cars was uneventful and silent. Even the rain had stopped. Once we were at the trailhead, we glanced at each other. We didn't need to say anything. I knew we were both thinking the same thing.

We had just met a ghost. We had always heard rumors of the trail being haunted, but we had never given any actual credit to those rumors. As we went to part ways, I looked at Kere. We made eye contact, and in that moment, we silently agreed that we would not share the events of the day. Let the ghost of the Lime Kiln remain a rumor, a figment of imagination. We both proceeded to get in our cars and make our journey home.

SASQUATCH HUNT

LUCAS JANKOVIC, WA.

Jamie woke up. He rolled over and saw his alarm clock. It read 10 AM. His eyes stung.

He wasn't used to waking up so early. He swung his legs over the side of the bed, landing his feet on the two spots of the carpet that weren't covered in junk. Most of the time, the floor was covered in dirty clothes, but the new junk was more expensive and less likely to be stepped on.

Jamie exited the bedroom. On his way to the kitchen, he smiled at his wife Emma, who was sitting on the couch. She did not smile back.

"Whatcha doing home, baby?" Jamie asked.

"Are you going today?" Emma asked.

Jamie paused. "It's a little late. Maybe tomorrow." Jamie grabbed a half-drunk gallon of chocolate milk from the fridge and drank directly from it.

"I took the day off," Emma said.

Jamie put the chocolate milk in the fridge and walked over to the couch. "What?"

"I took the day off. We're going up to the mountains and we're using the crap you bought," Emma said.

"But I'm not ready."

"It's been months."

"I don't have everything yet. I'm waiting on a portable shelter," Jamie replied.

Emma grabbed both of Jamie's hands, "I love you. I have spent over two thousand dollars on every piece of junk you asked for. I took the day off work, which pays for the junk. Get in the car."

Before Jamie knew what happened, he was behind the wheel of Emma's car, driving north. He packed as much gear into the sedan as possible, blocking the rearview mirror. Jamie was crunched into the front seat, not able to push his seat back for fear of breaking his equipment. His long legs were near his chest as he drove. The giant hands made the steering wheel look like a child's toy.

The beauty of the Pacific Northwest wasn't new to Jamie. He was born and raised on Whidbey Island, near where they were going. The sprawling forests and towering mountains didn't register as special anymore. He only missed his home once, when he went to college in Nevada. After two years there, he was ready to return, but after a month of being home, nature faded into the background again.

Emma was a different story. She had moved there five years prior from Nevada. She was used to the vast nothingness of the desert mixed with pockets of gambling. When the conversation arose about where they were going to live, Emma insisted on moving in with Jamie.

The second she set foot in Washington, she became transfixed by the landscape. Every chance she got was spent outside, climbing, hiking, whatever she could do to experience the new landscape.

After a while, the two were nearing their destination. Deception Pass. Even with his built-in apathy, Jamie couldn't deny the stunning nature that lay before him. The road leading up the pass was crowded by forests on both sides. Road signs teased viewing areas as they continued on, reaching the bridge.

The forest disappeared as the massive bridge rose over the waters of Deception Pass. Rushing seas flowed as far as the eye could see. Jamie and Emma spotted tree-covered islands on both sides, with small boats traveling between them. The rocky beaches down below led to a massive forest perfectly sculpted on the mountain in front of them. Cars lined the road, with passengers clambering for a chance to see the view.

"It's incredible," Emma said.

"You're right. He's here. I can feel it," Jamie replied.

"You can feel Bigfoot?"

"Yes, I can. It's a giant thing. You wouldn't understand."

The car reached the end of the bridge as the forest enveloped them once again. They continued on until reaching Deception Pass State Park. Jamie parked the car, and the couple climbed out of the vehicle.

"So, what are we bringing?" Emma asked.

Jamie opened the back seat, causing a crapalanche. "The camera, mic, headphones, ghillie suit, computer, crossbow, knife, net, testing sacks, carrying straps, first aid kit, and trail mix," Jamie said while pointing to each object.

"How much do I have to carry?" Emma asked.

"How about you grab the mic and the first aid kit. I'll be in charge of everything else." Jamie dropped his pants.

"Do I have to wear a ghillie suit?"

"You can wear the Bigfoot costume. I don't think it'll fit you, though."

"Yeah, I was gonna ask about that. Do you need to wear a Bigfoot costume for this?"

"Of course. That's the one thing every Bigfoot hunt is missing. They always come packing these huge camera crews and lights, but do they try to blend into the Sasquatch's natural habitat, no." Jamie said as he took his shirt off.

"So that's a yes on the ghillie suit?" Emma asked.

"You don't have to. Just like I don't have to get a job."

"If I put on the mud suit, you'll get a job."

"If we don't catch Bigfoot, I'll apply for a job."

Jamie was now down to his underwear when a ranger walked out of the woods. He was tall, with a long mustache and a Smokey Bear hat.

"Hello, folks. What . . . what are we doing here?" The ranger asked.

Emma felt more embarrassed for associating with Jamie than Jamie felt for being confronted by an officer of the law while nearly nude.

"No worries, officer. We're hunting Bigfoot. I'm sure you see this all the time," Jamie said.

"Of course. Ma'am, may I have a word with you over here? This will only take a minute." The ranger said as he led Emma away from Jamie.

"Don't take too long! Bigfoot is waiting!" Jamie exclaimed.

The ranger walked her far enough so that Jamie couldn't hear.

"Officer—"

"Ma'am. Are you safe?" The ranger asked.

"Of course. My husband is a bit eccentric when it comes to Bigfoot." Emma could see Jamie getting into his bigfoot costume.

"Does he think he is the almighty Sasquatch?" The ranger asked.

"No. He quit his job a while back. This is really all he has between him and my couch right now."

"I see. Last question. Does he wear that costume at home?"

"If he did, we wouldn't still be married."

"Good. If he gets too weird in that forest, give me a ring." The ranger handed Emma his business card.

"Will do. Thank you, officer."

Emma walked back to her husband as the ranger walked into the woods again. Jamie smiled at her as he held his rubber Bigfoot mask in his hands.

"What did he say?" Jamie asked.

"What do you think, Jamie?"

"Was it about the crossbow?"

"It's nothing. Give me the ghillie suit."

"Take off your clothes," Jamie said in a serious tone.

"No thanks," Emma replied.

"He'll smell you if you wear your normal clothes. That's why I taped a can of Axe and threw it in the suit before we left." Jamie gave his wife the ghillie suit. She instantly winced at the smell.

"Oh, God. So, he'll smell me but won't smell the gallon of body spray?" Emma asked.

Jamie paused, "Fine, you can keep your clothes on."

———

The two walked into the woods. It had been some time since Jamie breathed fresh air. He lumbered along, weighed down by the equipment and costume. He breathed heavily through the mask, making it slippery with sweat.

"Hey, you doing okay, hun?" Emma asked.

"What do you mean? I'm doing great!" Jamie lied.

"I believe you. You don't have to wear the mask, you know," Emma said.

"What if he sees me? I gotta blend in."

"What happens if we see Bigfoot?"

"Huh, the crossbow. I shoot him."

"Then what? He must weigh like five hundred pounds."

"If you were to read the manual I emailed, you would know that Eduard made sure that I bought these specialized Bigfoot carrying straps." Jamie pulled out a set of straps from his backpack and handed them to Emma.

"These are used to move a refrigerator," Emma said as she put the straps inside the ghillie suit, feeling guilty that Jamie had to carry the rest of the stuff.

"He is heavy. Believe me, I can feel his presence," Jamie said.

"Alright. Promise me you'll talk to me about exactly what you're buying next time," Emma said.

"Yeah . . ." Jamie said.

They continued on the maintained trail. The forest seemed to go on forever. In every direction stood trees as tall as the eye could see, with the forest floor covered with moss and logs.

As they walked on the trail, other hikers passed by them. They seemed to gawk at the costumed couple, with Emma hearing a few laughs behind their backs. Emma blushed in embarrassment, but Jamie barely noticed.

The couple rarely hiked together. Emma walked on with no problem, but Jamie was starting to show his exhaustion. Only an hour had passed since they started walking, and he was slowing down considerably. The two reached a juncture where the trail diverged into two paths. One way led towards the top of a cliff, with the other leading further into the woods.

"Are you ready to start heading back?" Emma asked, her own suit becoming unbearably wet with sweat.

"What? We drove all the way up here. We're not leaving. I know what's wrong, we're sticking to the path. Bigfoot isn't gonna be here with all the people smell. Let's pick a direction and go deeper." Jamie pointed away from the trail and started walking.

"Jamie, you've had your fun. You're out of breath and tired. It was a nice day. Let's take the win and go home," Emma said.

"You can wait in the car if you want. If I'm doing this, I'm doing it right. I never asked you to come here today." Jamie continued on. Emma followed.

As they walked off the trail, the weather began to change. The sunny day was replaced with cloud coverage. As a result, the forest became dimmer. Emma walked behind Jamie, pacing herself against his lumbering gait. In the low light, she could have sworn that he looked taller than he was. At 6'6, it was hard for her to keep track of how tall he was, with him slouching.

"Are you doing okay, Jamie? Let's take a break." Emma said, walking faster to catch up with him.

Jamie was panting. He walked to a nearby stump and sat down, taking off his gear. The weather had changed again. Fog began to roll into the forest.

"Here, let me," Emma said as she grabbed hold of his mask. It seemed to be stuck on his face, but with a few pulls, Emma ripped it off. The mask was dripping with sweat and condensation, and she set it down beside him.

"Are you okay?" Emma asked.

"Stop asking that. I'm fine," Jamie snapped.

"Geez, I'm just trying to help," Emma replied.

"No, you're not. You want me to give up, but it's not gonna happen."

"Do you honestly think I'm out to get you?"

"You sure as hell haven't been supportive."

"I don't know if you can see me, but I'm wearing a ridiculous outfit, same as you, which I bought, by the way. I've been nothing but supportive," Emma said.

"Is that why you dragged me out here? Support? Or is it that you thought I would give up and get a real job again?"

"I'm trying to understand you, Jamie. You quit your job, saying you want to explore hobbies and live life. I get it, that job sucked, but then you sit on your ass for a year. You say you want to hunt Bigfoot, so I buy you all the gear, and you don't go. What is happening with you?"

A roar echoed through the woods. Jamie and Emma quickly stood up. Jamie shook the sweat off the mask and put it back on. The fog obscured their view, but they could hear that the roar came from deeper in the forest.

"What was that?" Emma asked. "Oh no, don't say it."

"It's him. I can feel it in my soul. Bigfoot," Jamie said.

"Alright, I'm with you. I'll take the stuff, you go," Emma said. Jamie stood up and began walking towards the noise as Emma grabbed the crossbow and swung it around her back. The backpack was a struggle to put on, but Emma heaved it across one shoulder, holding on with both hands.

Emma jogged to catch up with Jamie. When she went by his side, he towered over her, more than usual. The silence was awkward. Emma wanted to continue the conversation that was interrupted, but the moment had passed.

"That costume makes you look taller," Emma said.

"You like it?" Jamie asked in a playful tone.

"I like your height. The gorilla suit, not so much," Emma replied.

"Yeah, this thing is getting uncomfortable." Jamie panted as he scratched his hairy midsection. It felt as though the suit was sticking to his skin.

"Just take it off," Emma said.

"I don't have any clothes on," Jamie replied.

"Oh, right. I forgot. At least take the mask off," Emma said.

Jamie grabbed the mask and pulled. It wouldn't budge.

"It's stuck!" Jamie exclaimed. He panicked and tried ripping the mask off, which caused him to yell out in pain.

"What is it caught on?" Emma asked.

"I don't know! It's glued to my face!" Jamie screamed.

"We should go back to the car! We can cut it off." Emma turned around and started walking away.

"There's a knife in the bag. Give it to me and I'll cut the mask off."

"We should really do this in the car, I don't want you to get hurt," Emma said.

"Wait. You were the one who took it off last time!" Jamie yelled.

"Yeah, you want me to try and take it off again?"

"No, you did this! You glued it to my face so we would go back to the car! Unbelievable!" Jamie swung his arms wildly around him. Emma had never seen her husband act this way. They had been in fights before, but he was never this unhinged.

"You're paranoid! We need to go."

"Paranoid? You want me to fail, don't you! You love being the one in control, the one who's always right! Emma and her bum husband!"

"It's easy to be right when I'm married to a crazy person!" Emma screamed back.

"You win! I'm a failure! You always win!" Jamie yelled.

He gripped the costume, trying to tear it off. He stumbled back, crashing to the ground. "Get it off me!" Jamie screamed.

Emma rummaged through the bag and found the folding knife.

"Jamie, I have the knife, sit still," Emma said.

"Give it to me! Get away!" Jamie yelled. Emma threw the knife on the ground in front of Jamie.

Jamie grabbed it, his giant hands fumbling with the knife. He brought the knife to the mask and stabbed it. Blood poured out. Jamie threw the knife away, roaring in pain. He grabbed onto the mask with both hands, curling into a ball.

Emma dug the first aid kit out of the bag and rushed to her husband's side. She shook her husband. The fur felt more real than it had minutes before.

"Show me the cut! I can fix it!"

"*ARGH!*" Jamie bellowed.

Jamie rose, now almost eight feet in height. He grabbed his head in frustration, trying one last time to rip off the mask, but it was one with his face, his mouth now being filled with giant, snarling teeth. His ape-like hands covered his eyes as he shook his head. A low growl escapes his mouth as his arms slowly drop to his sides. The stream of blood down his face slowed to a trickle.

Emma was frozen in place. She hoped this was all a nightmare, but the reality of the situation set in. Her husband, the one she loved most in the world, was now a monster. She looked into his blue eyes, the only part of him that still remained unchanged.

"Jamie? Are you still there?" Emma asked.

Jamie looked at her, and an inhuman growl roared, with him trying to form mangled words.

"Rrrr . . . Run!" Jamie screamed as his blue eyes were replaced with black orbs.

Emma screamed and turned around, sprinting away from the monster. The monster roared, sending chills down her spine. She pulled out her phone and remembered the ranger. She thought he had to be in the forest somewhere. She dialed the number on the business card.

"Hello, Deception Pass State Park Ranger's office, how can I help you?" She recognized the ranger's voice.

"I need help! My husband turned into Bigfoot!"

"Ma'am, is your husband hurting you?" The ranger asked.

"He's gonna kill me!"

"Can you make it to—"

The call dropped.

"No! No!" Emma yelled. She couldn't see more than 10 feet in front of her in the thick fog. There was no way of knowing if anyone still occupied the forest. She was alone.

Emma knew she could outrun Jamie, but the monster was another story. Emma took off the backpack, then the ghillie suit mask, throwing them against a tree. She could hear the creature's footsteps crunch against the forest floor. The sound was getting closer and closer.

Emma imagined what would happen once he caught up to her. Then, the noise stopped.

Emma slowed to a walk, looking back at the monster. He was distracted, picking up the objects she had left behind one by one, sniffing them. She knew that in a few seconds, he would get bored and begin chasing after her once more. She also knew that she could never outrun the monster at the pace he was chasing.

Emma slowly began taking off the ghillie suit, making sure not to make a sound. As she did, the straps she had put there earlier fell out.

Emma walked to a nearby tree and hung the ghillie suit on the tough bark, draping the empty sleeves over the branches. She kneeled behind the tree, tying the straps around as tightly as she could. She prayed that the monster would fall for her plan.

The monster raised its head, looking around the fog. He rose to his feet, smelling the air. He sprinted forward, following the scent. After a few seconds, he saw the source of the scent and lunged for it, using his arms to claw at the object in front of him.

Emma kept silent behind the tree as the sasquatch attacked the ghillie suit with ferocity. She winced at every strike, knowing that it could be her at any moment. Emma came out from behind the tree and threw the straps over the creature. He destroyed the ghillie suit, tying himself in the straps.

The monster was tangled, struggling against the tree, bashing his arms against the trunk. Emma got too close. He reached out as far as he could and swung his arms too fast for Emma to react, connecting with her side. She tried to scream, but the wind knocked out of her as she tumbled to the ground. Emma slowly got back on her feet, her body fueled by adrenaline.

She raised the crossbow, a bolt already loaded. Her hands trembled as she aimed the weapon at her husband's chest.

"Jamie! Please!" Emma screamed, even though she knew her husband was gone.

Emma knew Jamie would never hurt her, yet the monster had no reservations. The thought crossed her mind that if he were free, she would be torn apart without a second thought.

The Sasquatch struggled against the straps, swinging his giant arms wildly. He didn't react to her words. There was only rage at being subdued, the base animal instinct to survive, nothing more, nothing less. His black eyes stared at her with murderous intent.

Emma struggled to pull the trigger. Her husband had been with her minutes prior. He was there, talking, laughing, just like they always did. Could she really kill him, even though he had transformed into a monster? Tears streamed down her face, and her side ached with pain. Her life had changed in a matter of minutes without her realizing what she had lost.

After a few moments, she threw the weapon to the ground. She couldn't do it. The monster was freeing himself, steadily tearing through the straps with brute strength.

"Jamie, I'm sorry," Emma said quietly.

Emma ran away from the monster that was once her husband, gripping her side. As she arrived at the maintained trail, she could hear a roar in the distance.

THE LAST FEATHERS OF CROW ISLAND

BRITTANY TUCKER, WA.

I blinked against the blinding sunlight assaulting my eyes as I stepped off the schooner, the log-tied gangway swaying beneath my feet.

After stowing away for three months on a rum-running vessel, I could manage the rocking of the sea. The sun, though? It could shove right off.

My knees locked, unused to the stillness, as I crossed onto land. Dry land. Gloriously, wonderously dry land. By the heat beating on my skin, summer must have already begun. The endless supply of rum I'd been sneaking made it difficult to track the time.

A gruff, sweat-stained sailor knocked into my shoulder, pushing me off the small, plank dock and onto the beach. My boot slipped and I glanced down. Rocks. The entire beach was filled with barnacle-stained pebbles in all shapes and colors.

I'm far from home. Good. I wasn't going back.

The rustle of wings overhead made me pause. A glistening, black crow landed on the ship's mast. It cocked its head, clacking its beak, as its beady eyes locked on me. I watched it for a moment, the bird never averting its gaze.

Strange. I rolled my shoulders, turning away. I could still feel its eyes on my back.

Men shouted orders to each other as they unloaded crates and crates of liquor off the schooner. Just past the makeshift harbor was a long, narrow cabin, painted white with a sign over the door that read, *Office.*

Office for whom? As I slipped inside, I kept my head down, fighting to keep my gate steady. A red-bearded man with gigantic hands sat behind a crudely carved desk. Besides him, only a table and two chairs adorned the cabin.

The man blinked at me.

I blinked back.

His thick brows furrowed. "Are you lost?"

"Yes, actually." I pointed out the paneled window to where the glittering grey-blue sea lay beyond. "Where are we?"

"You come in on the rum-runner?" The man smirked slightly. Before I could answer, he continued, gesturing out the window. "*That* is the Puget Sound." He waved broadly over his head. "And you're on Crow Island, in the Washington Territory." Then he pointed at the floor. "Also, you're standing in my office, in the town of Utsaladdy."

"Ah," I replied. I still had no blasted idea where that was. "Well, I'm trying to start over. I'm sure I'm not the first. Is there work?"

"*Work?*" The man burst out in a belly laugh as he scooted away from his desk, the legs of his chair making an awful screeching sound. "Is there work, he asks. *Of course* there's work, you daft loon. Follow me."

I scowled but followed him outside. He clapped one of those meaty hands on my shoulder as he gestured toward the dense tree line, not two hundred yards away.

"Do you know what those are, boy?" he asked.

I made a face. "Trees?"

He smacked me across the ear. "Of course they're trees, you buffoon. What kind of trees?"

Rubbing my throbbing skin, I squinted, trying to get a closer look. The trees were tall, their limbs heavy with deep, green spines instead of leaves. That same crow—or at least it seemed to be—landed in one of the branches. It squawked as it watched me.

I swallowed and tried to shake away the queasy pit in my stomach. "D-Douglas Fir, is what they look like. We had them back on the farm."

"Very good," the man smiled, revealing yellowed teeth. "Do you know what we use fir for in these parts?"

I could imagine. "Logging, I assume. For ship building?"

"Logging for ship building," The man repeated as he nodded. He grabbed an axe off the porch and shoved it in my hand. "You want work? Meet me at the forest's edge in the morning. I'll put you to work." He handed me a couple of coins. "But for now, head on over to the tavern and find a bed and a hot meal."

"Thank you." I pocketed the coins. "I didn't catch your name?"

The man's veined, patchy cheeks paled as he glanced up at the sky. "Names aren't important around here, but if you must, call me Red."

He disappeared back into his office, leaving me alone outside. I turned, scanning for what he'd been looking at. A crow stared down at me, perched atop a stack of freshly cut logs. It flapped its wings, almost aloof, before it began to preen.

No wonder they call it Crow Island. That same uneasiness squeezed my insides as I shifted my attention to finding the tavern. It didn't take long. I merely had to follow the mixed, but equally exhausted, group of sailors and loggers to the two-story building on the west end of the town.

Utsaladdy. I reminded myself as I slipped in behind a ship-mate. The mouthwatering smell of bacon and fresh bread was as thick as a wall. I navigated through the crowd and managed to find a seat at the bar, but was disappointed to see, instead of a tavern wench, a lightly built barkeep with stringy, brown locks pouring drinks.

Without asking, he slid me a golden ale and said, "You're new." Not a question.

I nodded as I sipped, wiping foam from my overgrown mustache. "Just got in. Starting work with Red tomorrow."

"Are you?" The Barkeep's brow arched. "Well, best of luck, I suppose."

"What's that supposed to mean?" I braced my elbows on the counter. "It seems you'd have lots of passing strangers in a town like this."

"You'll be wanting a room?" he asked, ignoring my statement.

With a huff, I nodded and slid the coins across the counter.

"Keep them." The barkeep pushed them back, along with a thin, silver key. "Second door to the left. Head up after your meal."

Folks sure are bossy around here. I didn't want to start a fight, so I just nodded again. "Thank you."

As he turned away to serve the others waiting, I raised my hand to stop him. "Actually, I have a question."

He shot me a glare, but paused to listen.

I nodded toward the door. "What's with the crows?"

The barkeep's skin drained of color, just like Red's had. "What about them?"

"They don't seem frightened of people," I muttered, swirling my ale. "Thought it was odd."

The barkeep's smile was almost sympathetic. "Leave the crows be. Stay close to Red." He grabbed a fresh plate of bacon, eggs, cheese, and toast off the back counter and set it in front of me. "Eat, then go to bed, Newbie."

With that, he returned to his customers, leaving me with little appetite.

I woke the next morning with a black feather on my windowsill. It lay open, though I'd closed it the night before. I stared at the feather before finally pushing back my blankets. The chill in the air wrapped itself around my bones. I continued to stare as I dressed in the same filthy rags, the only clothing I owned. Before I left, I tucked it carefully into my pocket.

Perhaps it's an omen, I thought as I made my way to the forest's edge. For good or bad, though, I hadn't decided.

Like he'd said, Red waited for me beneath the fir boughs. He gave me a quick once-over as I approached. He nodded to the borrowed axe in my hand. "You know how to use that?"

"No, but I'm sure I can figure it out." I tossed it into the air, catching it a little too close to the blade. "I just hit the tree until it falls, right?"

Red grunted before striding into the forest. "You'll be a swamper, then."

"What's that?" I asked, following him beneath the canopy. Within moments, the trees enclosed us, smothering out the light and leaving us in a green-hazed gloom.

"You'll be clearing paths." Red gestured to the branches and underbrush we crunched beneath our feet. "You'll make sure we have an open space to drag the logs."

"Fine." I wanted to be offended, but decided to keep my mouth shut. "Sounds easy enough."

Red slowed as a tribble of piercing caws came from above.

He sniffed, "Nothing's easy around here. Keep your wits close."

I surveyed the trees, catching only a faint flash of black before the birds disappeared from view.

Several gruff voices became audible as we moved deeper into the woods—other workers. As they grew louder, the sounds were accompanied by the *zing* of saws and the sharp thuds of axes.

"How many men work for you?" I asked to keep the conversation going.

"Dozens," Red replied, "but they come and go. Just like you will."

"You don't know that." I huffed, tucking deeper into my tattered coat. "Maybe I'll stay on here and make a living in Utsaladdy. You're doing it."

Red gave him a wary look but didn't answer.

We rounded a bend in brush, revealing gigantic stacks of fir trunks, stripped of bark, and piled high enough to reach the surrounding firs' needles. Groups of equally burly men sat around the stack, sipping what smelled like coffee from thermos'. Break time.

"That way." Red nodded to a half-cleared path to the left of the work space, then handed me a smaller hand axe. "We lost our last swamper yesterday. Pick up where he left off. Keep clearing the route until you hit the beach. *Do not* wander into the forest. Stick to the path."

I took the tool and pressed it against my chest. "What happened to the previous guy?"

Red's smile was unnervingly wide. "He didn't listen."

"Oh." I wasn't sure how to respond to that. "What do I do once I reach the beach?"

"If you make it that far?" Red thought for a moment

before turning toward the group of men. "Enjoy the fresh air. Get started. Don't stop until sunset."

Don't stop until sunset. I shot him a frustrated look as he joined the others. *Don't go into the forest. Don't bother the crows. There's something off about this place.*

I couldn't stress about that now. I needed to earn a paycheck.

The path the previous swamper cleared stopped about one hundred feet from the clearing. I picked up where he left off, hacking away at the underbrush, my boots twisting in salal and blackberry bush groves. Within an hour, I was drenched in sweat. It leaked down my sides, chaffing them raw.

By the third hour, I was near vomiting from exhaustion. I'd grown rotund and out of shape on the rum-runner. I wasn't sure how far I could go.

I paused to catch my breath—my arms scratched and bleeding from the berry thorns. I'd come far enough that the men's voices were only fleeting vibrations through the foliage. Red wouldn't know if I took a quick break myself.

I slumped onto a fallen tree trunk, moisture instantly soaking through my ruined pants. Wide, orange mushrooms grew from the damp bark, dripping with dew.

Water. I hadn't brought any water.

You idiot. I let out a long sigh, wiping the sweat on my face onto my sleeve. I hadn't brought food, either. Nor had Red offered any.

I leaned back, closing my eyes, calmed by a gentle warbling in the distance. It took several moments for the realization to sink in—the sound was a stream.

What luck. I stood and looped my axe through my belt loop. Red said not to wander into the forest, but without water, I was useless. Besides, it was close if I could hear the stream this clearly.

A shadow flickered overhead as I took my first step off the path, onto the soft moss. A black feather gently fell to the ground at my feet.

My heart vaulted into my throat. *Not again.*

As my eyes rose to scan the treeline, searching for crows, another feather lay not far away, gently placed on a half-rotted stump.

What is going on? I wasn't sure why, but I grabbed the feather at my feet and tucked it into my pocket, beside the other. As I approached the stump and took the third, the forest seemed to hold its breath.

I held the three together, admiring them. They really were beautiful, almost glittering, in the dim light.

A loud squawk brought me back to attention.

A crow watched from the rusty orange branch of a Pacific madrone. Its dark eyes were unblinking, studying, waiting.

Waiting for what?

"Did you bring me these?" I held up the feathers. The crows stare didn't waver. I swallowed. The stream's babbling was louder. I was close. I gestured toward the woods. "I'll just get a drink, then I'll leave. How's that?"

The bird clacked its beak, rustling its wings.

I wasn't sure if that was a yes or a now, but my parched throat turned it into a fervent *yes.*

"Thank you." I took another step, my boot sinking deeper into the moss. "I'll be on my way, then."

It didn't move. It *watched* as I passed. I stepped over a slick ledge, glanced back, and found its beady black eyes boring into my back.

It's just a bird, I reminded myself as I picked my way down a short hill. Below, the stream came into view, its crystal clear water rushing over a worn pebbled bed.

It tasted even better than it looked. The brisk cold jolted

my blood awake as I swallowed. I let out a relieved sigh as I splashed my face, washing the sweat from my overheated skin.

A hoarse, grating rattle made my bones turn to stone.

I raised my head.

That very same crow watched me from across the stream. It breathed out another horrid rattle, the sound more man than bird.

"I'm leaving." I raised my hands, backing a step. "I'm leaving, I promise."

The crow's head slowly tilted. Its eyes, now more red than black, flickered to the treeline.

I followed its gaze.

Hundreds of crows—thousands of them—watched as I jolted away too fast, landing on my backside.

In one unified breath, they all began to rattle.

Screaming traveled through the twisting forest, a familiar shadow darkening it.

Red let out an irritated sigh, sinking his axe into a stump. "I guess we're going to need another swamper."

THE HAUNTINGS OF NEIHARDT HALL

SARA MOSIER, NE.

THE UNIVERSITY OF NEBRASKA-LINCOLN CAMPUS dates all the way back to the year 1869, one hundred and fifty-six years of collected memories. Good and bad, they seep into the very flesh of the land the school sits on. Most of the original buildings still stand to this very day, and with their continued existence comes the stories of their ghosts. Old Father, a place where a philosophy professor jumped to his death on the 10th floor in 1983 (records confirm this).

It has been reported that his spirit walks down the very hall leading to his former office, repeating the action of climbing over the edge of the window over and over. This has been seen by both students, staff, and professors, even though the windows are now locked and can no longer be opened on any of the floors. The Temple building, the original theater building, contains the restless beings of the thespian crowd, a set coordinator who had fallen to their death while it was under construction in 1906 has stuck around. He can be seen hovering from the rafters, calling out lines, playing notes of mysterious music, and flickering the lights off and on.

Of all the stories 156 years in the making, the ghost of

Neihardt Hall strikes a particular emotional chord. A polio outbreak occurred in the 1930s, housed within the walls where students were quarantined. The women were housed on the top floors, and the men on the lower level where the kitchen used to be. There are a few on record who passed away from all three of the diseases that caused lockdowns. A young woman haunts the 3rd floor, where previously there was the women's dorm room.

These ghostly stories made the campus headlines with the COVID-19 outbreak in 2020, similarly to the 1930s, students who were still living on campus were kept here in quarantine. It is not a wonder that this would stir up the ghosts of the past, with circumstances mirroring the panic and fear of an outbreak. A sobering reminder that modern medicine is a blessing, and those who stayed in the same rooms where people died, a hundred years later, feared the same fate.

Many students reported only hearing the voice of a woman, begging for help, scratching on the windows, and wandering the halls, looking for a way back home. Given the nature of the times, it is said she was either a nursing or teaching student from a small town who inadvertently took care of the sick. Unfortunately, she contracted (it is said polio) and passed within a few days from the fever.

Here is her story.

The ever-present dust caught in the steady current of sunlight seemed to glitter as it fell to the floor of the oak-paneled, walled room. It was a welcoming sight to revel in the rising of the sun, a new day, new possibilities.

The day began in usual silence, a short period of quiet just as the sun rose above the Nebraskan horizon. She could never see the actual rising of the sun. Her prison didn't allow this, but she could enjoy the filtered light that reached through the glass.

As mesmerizing as it was, the reality of her world was never too far behind to cast shadows. There were times when she forgot her name, as the day reached its end, something happened. She could never pinpoint it, as each night began to wane, the world from another time, the wailing, the crying, the acceptance of death would fall silent. Each mounting minute until the clocks would strike two, she was back in the hospital. It wasn't a lively dormitory, brimming with the chatter of fellow women students. It was a makeshift battleground against an invisible enemy, stealing those away in the night who didn't survive the first house of the fever.

First light made everything different. It was within these precious moments that she remembered her days as a girl, before arriving at the University to study literature. She would cling to the carefree remnants of her first days of college, her future unsure and exciting. The world at her feet, and taking every open door. All the bright and warm days before the outbreak seemed like a lost memory out of reach.

Her literature studies soon turned to medical, or at least as much as a woman was allowed to know, she surpassed the knowledge of even some of the doctors on campus. With quarantine, what else was she to do? Initially, she had never wanted to be a nurse, never wanted the burden of children, yet here she was tending to the sick and dying. Something expected of her, she supposed, because of her sex. Coming from a large family, it came as second nature, but she resented it, she hated it, she doubted very much that she brought much comfort to those dying from polio. At the time, there was no room for the sexual divide, and she tended to both men and women as the population of the sick began to rise at an alarming rate.

It was inevitable, really, that she might join the ranks of the sick. She never thought it would be with those dying. She couldn't remember falling sick. Had it still been spring? It had become a disastrous blur, to bed with a fever, her body immobilized within a few days. If someone were to have asked her, When did you die? She was never sure if she could answer it truthfully. It was easier to lie, act shocked, pretend it wasn't true. As it was, she was more often alone than not, so the problem of long conversations never came to be.

Anne never understood why she ruled the daylight in this building. The third floor where she remembered briefly there had been dorms, once places of laughing, studying, and planning for the future, only to become places of death. Last words. Last goodbyes. Her best friend and roommate had become her nurse. After Anne passed into this prison, she never saw her friend again.

She preferred the day when she could pretend it was like it was before. Go about her studies, walk the grounds, and get fresh air. Once nighttime came, all of those things were cast aside. With the sun's setting came the veil's piercing, it would fall down to the foundation of the building, and her world was open. She felt all at once the oppressive feeling of overcrowding slough away. It highlighted how alone she was, but at least no one was calling her name, begging for help, and writing letters to families of those who didn't survive.

The odd thing about being dead, among many things, was that she felt like she was in her very own ghost story. Her own haunted home. So many of the other occupants, former patients, a particularly loud young man on the ground floor, hardly ever noticed she existed. The nurses she had seen in her first days here stayed together. They always wore medical clothes, long white skirts and bonnets, attire far older than what Anne had worn. They were long dresses all the way down past their feet, inconvenient, and she was almost sure they were made out of wool. They could have been nuns, she was never sure, but their presence didn't last. It was as if they arrived together and left together, but she wasn't sure.

The passage of time was confusing. She had long since given up on any explanation of why she was stuck in this foreign state of limbo. This odd afterlife that never changed, the world outside the high windows at the entrance gave her glimpses of the last moments of her life on the outside. The thing was, she couldn't leave, as if an invisible tether sewn into her gut kept her from wandering away from the grounds. More times than she could count, in the early days of her arrival, she would scream for someone, anyone, for help, for answers. When she received no reply, she simply screamed. She'd throw herself through the bright white doors of the foyer, so bright they illuminated with cold light. She could feel the brick underneath her heels, catching and threatening to topple her over as she fled the place of death.

Then it would happen. She knew deep down in her soul that she was merely inches away from her escape before the ground beneath her gave way. As if getting pulled into a river's sink hole, sucking her up with such force she didn't know which way was up or down. She kept running, but instead of running outside and past the pillars on the front steps, she was running inside into the hall. Into the foyer, lit dimly, the daylight gone, and only the darkness to greet her.

It had frightened her so badly that she never tried that again, whether it was death or the invisible tether that kept her bound, she didn't want to figure out either way. The other people around her never had answers, nor did any of them recognize when she spoke. There were only a few rare moments when she would see the man, an odd walking torso that terrified her, and a myriad of faceless students from several different centuries of time.

Today was her usual schedule, and as she retreated to the attic once the sun set, something was different. Even going through the motions that never changed, she could feel the shift in the energy of the inside. She wasn't just feeling a distant buzz of human life around her, and the occasional passing through of a person, or a voice that would echo from nowhere. This was different.

The building looked the same as it always did once it grew dark, the gaslight lanterns would come on, one by one like sprouting flowers, but there was a cluster of voices. They were in the room with her, here in one of the staff rooms with the wooden walls and maroon carpet.

The veil keeping her separated from a multitude of occupants, the living and breathing intruders were crossing through that veil, piercing it, and the voices were no longer muddled. They were asking questions, one after another. They were clear and sharp. They hurt her ears as she covered them with her hands. The voices of the living were always a shock that left her dizzy.

There was a short, stout woman who looked to be the age of her own mother. Her image flickered in and out as if it were a moving picture.

"If there's anyone here with me now, can you move close to this little black box here?"

She did indeed produce a small box; she moved closer without thought to get a better look, and it began to scream in a high, shrill tone that made her cover her ears again.

"Don't let that frighten you, it's supposed to make that noise. That means I know you're here."

Anne scoffed. "Well, of course I'm here." She so rarely spoke aloud, even while she was by herself, her voice sounded grating from disuse. There was a fleeting and horrifying thought, in the midst of an ungodly high fever, she remembered she could no longer speak, barely above a whisper to beg for water, ice, anything to smother the heat and thirst.

"Is there anything that you'd like to tell us? Something to say? Is there a reason you haven't moved forward into the afterlife?"

Anne crossed her arms and gritted her teeth. She wasn't exactly sure why she was becoming angry, but she was. Who was she, this faceless and unnamed woman, and who gave her the right to ask any questions at all?

"This is the afterlife, are you joking? This is all I have known, every day of my existence.

You stay in whatever small place you perish and wait. Now, given that I've been here for more time than I am able to count, not properly anyway, without a clock, but I've been here long enough to know this seems to be all there is."

If this woman heard her, she never gave any kind of indication. She was fiddling around with another object that looked like a metallic kitchen tool. "We can see later if we got anything."

Oh, Anne thought, there's more than one of them this time. They ask me to say something, to make them hear me, see me, feel me, and yet I'm talking to myself.

"How many are here with us now?" another woman asked, this one far younger, more than likely a student. "I've seen a woman more than once, she walks around the third floor or maybe the attic, I'm not sure. She seems to be the strongest spirit here, is that correct? I was told the third floor was the main area to keep quarantined students. Were you a nurse here during the polio outbreak? The measles?"

She took immediate notice of the young woman speaking. It was startling, like looking into a mirror. She hadn't seen herself in so long, she wondered if she looked disheveled, if her hair was still combed neatly into a bun, and if her dress was still free of wrinkles. She refrained from moving closer, simply staring at this new person, as the lights flickered like a dying candle. This garnered a reaction from her visitors.

Now the stout woman with the tools was speaking to the other. "Have you ever seen the ghost you call Anne? Like, actually seen her in full form?"

The girl shook her head, hugging her own body as if to cradle herself. "No, but I hear voices and walking. The room next to mine, before anyone moved in. I thought someone had already moved in for the Fall semester. Things are so crazy here when classes start, I didn't think to ask. That is, until someone moved in, and that's when I started to wonder who the hell had been in the room next door. It had been locked up since last spring, and no one cared to tell me. I've only heard noises."

She finished as she cleared her throat and wrung her hands. She was trembling as if cold. "Sometimes I can feel her . . . when she's upset. Or at least she must be. I've just never talked about it. This is my first time on a big campus, and I don't wanna be the girl who sees ghosts."

"Darcy, are you sure you've never seen her before? I can see a faint image of her, and I think I know why you keep hearing her, sensing her. She looks a lot like you. Same dark hair and hazel eyes, about the same height too."

It was like being shoved. Suddenly, all three of them were in the courtyard.

"A couple of the other girls said they've seen a guy here, with a mop or a broom, sometimes he's even out here. We hear names floating around, whether people made them up, I'm not sure, but we call him Henry. And well, the uh, the torso? I've never seen it, thank god, but uh, we haven't named that, him, her, uh, them."

"One of the forgotten bodies, perhaps? From the graveyard that was here before?"

The girl now known as Darcy only shrugged. "I mean, I don't know. Again, it's one of those things you read about but are never sure if it's real or not. I'm from Bennet, it's a little bit North of here, so I didn't grow up here. I guess this is a pretty big hotspot, and some think it's the graveyard, or the fact that it was always a quarantine building for several outbreaks, polio, tuberculosis, influenza, and even COVID. There weren't a lot of happy things that happened here." She pointed towards the third floor with the oval-shaped window. "That was Anne's room, also my room, supposedly she died in there."

Anne looked back at the building she now called home. She was standing alongside these two very alive people as if they were simply all having a chat in the courtyard. Surely, they didn't see the fog that encased the entirety of the property. It was perpetual.

"You never see fog?" Anne thought to say out loud. "Even now?"

The older woman her eyes were still around the yard, but Darcy's were sharply locked onto Anne. "Did you hear that?"

The older woman seemed to be ignoring her.

"I don't see any fog now, but when it rains, it kinda comes out of nowhere out here."

Darcy replied, her arms falling away from her body, one hand sweeping outward, her eyes never moving. "Do you see it all the time?"

Anne had the overwhelming need to begin weeping. Besides the occasional passing between spaces with the other occupants, this was the first time someone was replying to her.

"Yes. Always . . ." Anne continued slowly, the urge to reach out overpowering. "I think it's what keeps me here. What an odd thing, the idea that fog can be the cage."

"Why are none of these things acting up?" Darcy spoke sharply, pointing to the devices in the other woman's hand. "I heard her and I think I saw her."

"I see you too, don't go, not yet, please." Anne trembled, following closely behind the young woman, her hands hovering, clenching, and unclenching her fists. She wanted to scream.

"You saw me, you were speaking right to me!"

The bursting sound of glass filled the gaps of silence. The courtyard fell away like discarded dishwater.

Anne now stood inside alone, only seeing the yard from the ornate third-floor window. The building was dark, she must have made the ceiling bulbs break again. That was a sure-fire way to get the privacy she usually craved. Not this time, no, she wished she had paid more careful attention so she could replicate how she'd been able to make true and honest contact.

Everything was like it was before. There were no distant voices, no blurred edges of the past. Whatever this person brought with them, they seemed to flee with it as well.

Once more, it was night, the white glow of the moon bleeding through the curtains of her third-story room. "Me, myself, and I," she murmured brokenly.

There on the windowsill, where the moon shone in, there was a small mason jar, old and ornate. A few coins at the bottom, a notebook, and a pen beside it. She stood up from where she had slumped.

She reached out her hand, the glass was smooth and cold, she swallowed a gasp as it fell onto its side. One by one, she lined the coins up, then stacked them into neat little piles. Had they always been here? Had the girl left them behind? Had the time passed already, days, weeks, months? She could never be sure.

Thereupon, the notebook, written in careful cursive letters, read.

> *"If you're ever feeling lonely. I left these things for you and only you. I hate the thought of my great-grandmother still trapped here. If you can read this, and I hope you can, know that you are not truly alone. The woman I was with said the coins may help you tell what year it is. The other girls on the floor know. These things will always be here."*
>
> *With Love,*
> *Darcy*

Would this be her doorway home? To the other side? To where her family waited? For the first time in what she now knew was almost a decade, she felt the air around her less oppressive. If she listened close enough, she could hear the campus bell ringing, and it rang past the hour of 2 am, her death hour. Time was moving forward. She could sense it now. Maybe she could also follow its magnetic pull, like the waves following the tides.

LEGEND OF THE FAERY STONES

KELLY CRUMPLEY, WA.

Claire didn't mind being alone because the faeries kept her company.

In fact, she preferred to be in the presence of faeries or animals over people. Her schoolmates considered her odd, but what they didn't know was that Claire was saving the last of the faeries with her garden in the forest. Her parents were too busy themselves to ever notice that Claire was in and out of the house doing secret things for the faeries. And this worked just fine because the fewer people who knew about the faeries, the safer they were.

But Claire didn't always know the faeries. In fact, the faeries watched Claire for a long time before ever giving her a faery stone so she could see and talk to them. Faeries from various ranks within their clan would come to watch her to see if she could be trusted.

They liked the way Claire observed the world around her. The way she was intrigued by the way the morning light came through her window and scattered however it wished, never the same way twice. How she marveled at the little rainbows it created on certain days and touched in the most random places in her room, sometimes dancing and moving, although she couldn't always quite determine where the light was reflecting from, so as to see why it would change shapes and move around. Dancing lights were welcomed guests in the girls' eyes, the kind of girl who noticed the little, beautiful things in life that most people passed by without a second thought.

The faeries decided that a human like this was safe to talk to, especially since she was the one who planted flower seeds in the forest.

Back then, Claire had been collecting flower specimens and planting exotic seeds in hopes of cultivating a beautiful collection of cut flowers, colorful vegetables, and maybe fruits, if she was lucky.

She always saved a few seeds after planting, which went in her seed pouch, in the original packet, so that she knew what they were and how to plant them. She had quite the collection of little seed envelopes and packets shoved in her top dresser drawer, seeds from all over the world that her Aunt Kara sent her in the mail every holiday.

Claire was a girly girl who wore princess dresses every day, but she also loved to get her hands dirty, causing her mother to sew her an apron to protect her clothes.

Claire experimented making her own soil and substrates, sprouting her tiny seeds, watering them, making sure they had enough light, and then selecting just the right spot for them in her forest garden. Which, really, wasn't hers. It was simply a sunny bit of land in the forest, which she hiked to every morning to tend before school. It was hard work preparing the ground and clearing stumps, raking hard ground sometimes, and bringing in bags of compost and softened bricks of coco choir to amend the soil.

Claire planted showy milkweed, purple butterfly bushes,

pink and red zinnia, coneflowers, aster, bee balm, verbena, goldenrod, calendula, and snap dragons.

The faeries watched all of this, and finally, it was decided that Claire could be even more helpful if she knew about them.

Queen Aria of the faeries also thought, although she never told anyone, that Claire could use the company, worried that she might turn out to be odd if she didn't make any friends. It was a very exciting day for the butterfly faeries when it was announced that they would give Claire a faery stone and show themselves to her.

And so, one morning, Maple and Birch flew through Claire's open window, placed a faery stone on her windowsill, then hid behind a pot of calendula flowers to wait. Sure enough,

Claire was dazzled by the light of the morning sun hitting her crystal chandelier, and her eyes landed sleepily on the stone. Her brows crinkled as she squinted, trying to see what strange object sparkled on the sill. She tossed back her covers and trudged over to the window and picked up the smooth, little white stone, turning it over carefully in her hand.

"She's got it now!" Maple giggled and flitted her wings. Claire stopped in her tracks, her eyes scanning the room for the source of the sound. Two butterflies with bodies of tiny humans emerged from behind a plant and fluttered in front of her. There was a female with red hair and a green dress holding a bundle in her arms, and a male, a bit bigger, with a scruffy beard and a wild mop of fiery red hair.

Claire's eyes widened in amazement as she whispered, "Hello there! Are you real?" she asked softly, so as not to frighten them away.

"Yes, we're real Miss Claire! We have been watching you closely in the forest with your plants, and we have come to say thank you! Look! The first faery baby born in many years!

Thanks to your garden of wildflowers and milkweed, we and our babies finally have food to eat."

Claire looked at the little bundle, which was wrapped in wide blades of soft grass. "Well, that's . . . that's wonderful!"

Maple carefully gave the bundle to Birch. Her eyes sparkled with excitement as she wagged her finger at Claire. "It's more than wonderful. It's a miracle, Miss Claire. The faeries are dying. We are the last clan left. Someone has killed all the milkweed, and our babies are very particular. It is the only food they will eat. Where on earth did you find milkweed seeds?"

Wracking her brain, Claire pondered this question. There was only one place rare, unknown seeds would have come from: her dear Aunt Kara. She knows every leaf, flower, tree, and blade of grass. Being around her is to love her, because she is always doing something useful.

She taught Claire and her sister, Emma, how to find their way through a night in Ebonshire Forest on a new moon, and she's also as wild as the wind, never following the rules and always doing something that would get her into trouble.

"Most likely from my Aunt, why?"

"Well, if anyone finds out about us, we could be in grave danger!" Maple says, flitting her wings nervously.

"Oh my Aunt won't cause you any trouble. She may have planted some at her house, too! She's just a few hours away by train."

Maple and Birch locked eyes, and Maple began pacing.

"This means there could be more faeries beyond Camano Island," Birch said thoughtfully, then cradled his bundle and looked at Claire. "Will you help us expand the garden, Miss Claire? The soil here is parched and dry and full of rocks. We need more amendments. We need more than compost, old leaves, and scraps of fruit and vegetables—we need manure from animals!" He said excitedly.

"Manure? You mean . . . animal poop? Really?" Claire gasped in disgust.

Maple and Birch both nodded. They looked at Claire, hoping she would agree, for the faeries could only do so much on their own, and carrying heavy loads was not something they could do with such low numbers. If only they could grow their clan large enough to sustain themselves. They desperately needed the girls' help.

Claire, being a kind and helpful girl, could not turn them down. In fact, although she didn't like the idea of working manure into her garden, she did like the idea of expanding it and making her flowers happy.

"Sounds like we'll need a wheelbarrow for this job," Claire announced most seriously.

The faeries squealed with happiness, accidentally waking the caterpillar, who joined in the fun, making tiny cooing sounds.

"Thank you, Miss Claire! Now keep the faery stone with you all the time so that we can talk with you! You mustn't tell anyone about us, Miss Claire. You must swear an oath!"

Claire held the faery stone tightly in her hand, feeling its warmth and magic pulse through her fingers. "I, Claire, solemnly swear to keep the existence of the faeries a secret. I vow to protect their home and their lives with all my heart. I promise never to reveal their presence to anyone, no matter the circumstances. This oath I take willingly, with the faery stone as my witness, and the forest as my guardian. May the magic of the faeries remain hidden and safe, forever."

"Perfect!" Maple exclaimed with an approving nod, tossing her long red hair.

Claire went into the bathroom she shared with her sister and got dressed quickly, then slipped the faery stone in her pocket while the faeries waited in her bedroom. In her mind, she worked through all the ideas that were whirling through her mind.

Claire emerged from the bathroom and padded over to where Maple and Birch fluttered happily by the window. "Okay, I'll need a couple of days to gather everything. I'll ask my father to help fix the wheelbarrow. It's got a flat tire. But he can fix anything, so that shouldn't be a problem. My big concern is where we'll find manure."

"Can you call any local farms? They might sell it to you." Birch suggested.

"But how would I buy it? I don't have any money. Well, never mind, let me figure that out." Claire decided.

Claire got out her notebook and pen and started making a list of all the farms in town.

At school, she asked around, gathering phone numbers, and to her delight, a quiet girl named Shawna, who always had her nose in a book, said her family has horses and might give some away for free, but that she had to ask her parents after school. Claire went to school excited the next day, because she couldn't wait to hear what Shawna had to say. And sure enough, they offered the manure, and even offered to deliver it if she took a whole trailer full. However, as excited as Claire was, she had to go home and ask herparents if it was okay to have a giant load of poop delivered.

Considering her parents weren't much of gardeners, she was concerned they wouldn't understand. But Claire's father was kind and loved Claire's flowers. So when Claire brought it up, and assured him that she intended to move it out of the driveway, and into the forest quickly, he offered to fix the wheelbarrow all on his own. Claire was so relieved and happy. Her father removed the flat tire and put on a new one, then wrapped the wooden handles with leather so Claire wouldn't get splinters.

The next day, the trailer was delivered, and Claire got to work. Her father left her a nice big shovel, too.

Claire would push the loads across the backyard, through the gate, and would disappear into the forest. She only had time to move three loads before school without getting too sweaty. After her homework and house chores were done, she dashed outside to keep working.

Every day, she'd bring something new to decorate the faery grotto—a string of beads left over from a party, a piece of her grandmother's old costume jewelry, colorful glass gems, painted wooden mushrooms, and little carved animal figurines she thought the faeries might like. And even though butterflies preferred to sleep hidden in bushes and brush piles, Claire painted several little faery-size doors and propped them up against the base of tree trunks. The little white pebble created a lump in Claire's pocket.

Claire was faithful to always keep it with her so the faeries could talk to her. Tufu, her bird, who was a huge gray harpy eagle her father brought home one day as a rescue, helped carry tools and loads of whatever 'magical dirt' Claire thought was needed at any given time. The bird was a great help because he never complained about all the various things she needed, like worm castings and moss, lime from the quarries, and manure from the giant pile that was shrinking slower than Claire would have liked.

Claire even asked her family to collect food scraps to make compost for dirt to feed the faery garden.

To water everything, Claire dug grooves in the ground coming from the creek all the way to the sunny garden glen. The water flowed downhill at just the right angle making every-thing grow. All the while, the faeries kept her company and brought her red clover nectar to drink, big blackberries to eat, and woven daisy crowns.

Claire worked long hours every day to get it all done, and even though she was tired and dirty at the end of the day, she never felt better. Claire was saving the faeries. But as the days drew on, Claire's little sister grew more and more agitated, lonely, and suspicious. She started spying on Claire and even followed her into the forest one day.

Even though Emma didn't have a faery stone to see and talk to the faeries, to her, the faeries just looked like regular butterflies. She could hear Claire talking to them.

It took about a month for another patch of showy milkweed to grow. The pretty pink and white clusters of star-like flowers swayed in the gentle summer breeze, and Claire checked under the leaves to check for butterfly eggs, just like the faeries had instructed her.

When the caterpillars hatched, Tufu would keep watch to make sure no other birds would eat the babies before the mother faeries would come and wrap them in soft grass and make them beds in the snapdragons. Claire would help with this each night, squeezing the sides of the blossoms while the faeries would place their babies inside to sleep.

The butterfly faeries tended the garden while Claire was at school or with her family, and pulled weeds as they sprang up, picked off dead leaves and old brown flowers, and kept the water irrigation lines clear from debris. Windstorms were always blowing things around and causing a mess in the forest, and then in their garden, dropping limbs and leaves in unwanted places. So those all went to the mushroom beds where they could be utilized. Claire's mushroom beds were getting bigger every year.

One mushroom had basically grown so big, there was a huge clearing in the forest where the mushroom had eaten all the trees over the years, and it had baby mushrooms popping up in a huge ring. The mushrooms as babies were honey yellow and a bit sweet. Claire collected them, chopped them up, and cooked them with lots of butter, a little honey, and cinnamon for her family. The faeries told her that mushroom rings only grow where there are faeries, and that, besides faery stones, this was the only other place you could go to talk to the faeries.

After three long years, Emma couldn't stand it anymore. One day, she found sketches of faeries in Claire's notebook.

"I knew it!" Emma said to herself. She was tired of watching her sister tend her garden so happily. She wanted to be friends with the faeries too. And, she wanted her sister back.

Emma didn't want to be a thief, but when Claire left the faery stone on the counter in the bathroom, Emma couldn't resist. She slipped it into her pocket. And when Claire ran back into the bathroom, panicked, looking for the stone, Emma stayed quiet. And although the guilt weighed on Emma's heart, she didn't say a word, and she didn't give it back. But it didn't work for Emma the way it worked for Claire. Everything was just as before for Emma, but not for Claire.

When Claire went to tend the garden before school, no faeries greeted her. No babies were inside the snapdragons to wake up for the day. All she saw were butterflies flitting wildly in the sunny glen. Claire wondered if losing the faery stone made the faeries not want to talk to her anymore. She was sad and angry at this thought. After all she did for them, how could they ignore her like this? They were her friends. Her only friends. Claire felt so alone, so she ran, tears streaming down her face, to sit in the center of the faery ring of mushrooms in hopes of seeing the faeries one last time.

As soon as she stepped into the ring, the faeries filled the ring and surrounded her.

Unbeknownst to Claire, Emma watched from deep in the forest.

"Don't cry, Miss Claire! We would never forget you!" The

faeries fluttered around her, whirling into the air in a kaleido-scope of colors, swirling into shapes of animals to make Claire laugh.

"What happened to my faery stone?" Claire asked, swiping a tear from her face.

Her best friend, Maple, answered, "I hate to be the one to tell you this, Claire, but Emma took your faery stone."

Claire's heart dropped. "That dirty, thieving brat!"

Queen Aria approached Claire, the other faeries parting the way to let her through. Her pretty pink gown, which reminded Claire of a peony, flowed gently behind her. "Miss Claire, don't be angry with her."

"Oh, I'm angry! Why shouldn't I be angry? I have every right to be angry!"

The Queen smiled and landed on a mushroom, tucking her wings behind her. "You have every right to be angry, but holding onto that anger will only hurt you more. Your sister misses you, and she has been spying on you. She knows about our garden and has also found your sketches. She wants to be friends with the faeries, too. You can hardly be mad at her for that."

Claire's eyes locked with the Queen's. Maple and Birch both looked at Claire tenderly.

"Well, no, I guess I can't blame her for that, now can I?" She admitted with a laugh. "Well, what do I do? I must get the stone back."

"Emma can't see the faeries just because she stole a stone," Birch hollered, "Only those who earn the trust of the faeries can have a stone! We can not make exceptions, even for Claire's sister!"

All eyes landed on Queen Aria, who was now sitting, deep in thought. Murmurs broke out between the faeries. Claire slumped down, sprawling back into the grass and staring up at the fluffy white cotton-candy clouds that danced across the blue sky. After a few minutes, Claire sprang up with an idea tickling her mind.

"What if my sister helped with the garden? Could she earn a faery stone? She already knows about you anyways. And with her help, we could work twice as fast!"

The Queen snorted at this idea.

"Oh, please, Queen Aria? Little Emma isn't a bad child. She made a mistake, yes, but everyone makes mistakes. We can teach her how to earn her own stone!" Maple said fervently.

The Queen looked at all the faeries. "We must all decide this together, it is very risky. It is not just my decision to make."

The faeries did not have time to decide.

From the shadows of a red elderberry tree, Emma watched her sister speaking to herself within the circle of mushrooms. Even though she couldn't see the faeries, she knew they were there, talking about her, for she had heard Claire use her name along with the rough side of her

tongue. She knew she shouldn't dare move, but something in her ached to chase after her sister and the faeries. Emma emerged from her hiding place and ran into the circle.

Claire screeched at the sudden movement, but immediately recognized her sister. The faeries did not stay. They fled the ring and left Claire and Emma standing alone together. Claire wasn't sure if she should be upset or apologize. Emma did steal her faery stone, but it was because Emma was lonely and wanted to see the faeries, too. Claire hated keeping secrets from her own family. It was a terrible thing to do, and everything in her wanted to tell them. She decided to apologize in hopes of reconciliation, and so that her sister would give back the faery stone.

Claire ran to her sister and wrapped her arms around her. "I'm sorry I couldn't tell you about the faeries, Emma! I was bound by an oath! No one can know about them. They show themselves to whom they wish. I hope you can forgive me for keeping this secret from you. I never meant to hurt you, I have just gotten so carried away with trying to save the faeries, that I have forgotten my own family!"

Emma squeezed Claire tightly, then drew back and looked her in the eye, "I'm sorry I stole your stone, Claire, I didn't mean to take you away from your faery friends, I just wanted to be friends too. I miss you!"

"I know Emma, I know! It's alright! We will figure this out, together." Claire said, taking her sister's hands and squeezing them.

One by one, the faeries fluttered back into the faery ring, revealing themselves. Their orange and black wings were framed by black and white polka dots. Their skin varied in all colors from creamy white to rich brown and every shade of caramel in between. Their hair was all hues of red, but varied from bright tangerine orange to deep cherry wood. The soft flutter of tiny wings could barely be heard over the murmurings from the faeries.

A smile cracked on Emma's face, spreading ear to ear as she observed the faeries for the first time. Claire stood proudly as all the young faeries inspected Emma with great interest.

"If you hold very still, one might land on your finger!" Claire said softly, sticking out her index finger. Maple landed on it and flitted her wings with a grin. Lacing her tiny fingers behind her back, she paced back and forth on Claire's outstretched finger.

Emma mimicked her older sister, and Birch landed quickly, but Emma squawked so loudly with delight that it scared him away. With a frown, Emma tried again, and Birch circled cautiously a few times.

Maple put her hands on her hips. "Oh, come on, Birch, she was just excited, give her a break!"

Birch landed again with a huff, puffing out his chest as a show of strength. The girls couldn't help but laugh again, but this time, Emma did it quietly.

Queen Aria came forward with a somber look on her face, "Hello Emma, I'm Queen Aria, and these are the butterfly faeries. Your sister has been helping us and needs her faery stone. It will only work for her anyways. It was very wrong of you to steal it. If you want to be friends with faeries, you must earn your own faery stone!"

"I'm sorry, Queen Aria. Truly, I am. Is there anything I can do to earn my own stone?"

"I can not even think about that yet, first, you must return Claire's stone at once!"

Without hesitating, Emma fished the faery stone out of her pocket and handed it to Claire.

Queen Aria twirled the ruffles on her dress and flew so close to Emma's face that she had to take a step back. "You are forgiven for stealing, but now you must show us that you are trustworthy. You haven't gotten off to a very good start, but we all make mistakes. I suppose if you are willing to help us in the garden . . . yes, that will work! We will give you a faery stone, but this isn't all fun, Miss Emma. Claire has been working very hard alongside us to save our species. If you take the stone, it's because you genuinely want to help, too. You must keep it with you all the time and you can not lose it. If, by the end of the summer, you have made a true and honest effort in the garden, you will be considered a friend of the faeries and may keep the stone. How does that sound to you?"

With a curtsy, Emma replied, "That sounds very fair, Queen Aria! Very fair indeed!"

So, the faeries celebrated, and Claire and Emma went home

that night and stayed up late talking about the faeries. In the morning, when it was time to wake the baby caterpillars, Emma jumped out of bed, washed, dressed, and ate quickly, and followed her sister silently into the forest to help. Emma had soft hands and a kind heart, and the faeries all learned to love Emma just as much as they loved Claire.

Claire was so thankful to have the help, and it was fun to teach her sister all about the faeries and the plants. That summer, the sisters grew closer than they had ever been, and the two became inseparable. And when Claire got a summer cold and couldn't get out of bed, Emma faithfully did her chores, so the faeries and flowers were cared for.

When the summer was drawing to an end, and the leaves were crunchy on the ground, the Faery Queen paid them a visit as they were trimming back the flowers of high summer. She carried a bouquet of dandelion flowers and two dandelion puffs. "Good morning, girls!"

"Good morning, Queen Aria!" They chimed together.

"I just wanted to come and personally thank you for your help this season. Our clan is stronger than it's ever been, and it's all thanks to you two. I brought you both a gift!"

"This has been the most wonderful summer ever! I've never worked harder or been happier!" Emma exclaimed triumphantly.

Pride swelled in Claire's chest. "I'm thankful for your help, Emma, but I'm more thankful to have you as my best friend."

The Faery Queen beamed. "I'm so proud of you both. I have brought you Story-Teller Flowers so you can each make a wish. It is our way of saying thank you!"

Emma gave a confused look. The Queen handed each of the girls a dandelion puff. "You may know Story-Teller Flowers as dandelions . . . Dandelions tell the story of the sun, moon, and stars!" Queen Aria began, "The yellow flower is the sun, the puff is the moon, and when you make a wish on the puff and blow the seeds into the air, they are the stars! Everyone knows that stars go shooting through the sky when you are granted a wish. Now, think of your wish and blow on the puff. But you mustn't tell anyone your wish, or it won't come true. You must keep it locked in your heart and mind. Go on, make a wish!"

So the girls made wishes, sending the fluff to dance in the wild wind. And as the summer drew to a close, Claire and Emma's bond grew stronger, and the faery garden flourished under their care. The faeries, grateful for the sisters' dedication, promised to watch over them always.

And so, the legend of the faery stones continues to thrive on Camano Island. To this day, if you are gardening or wandering through the forest, listen closely- you might hear the faint flutter of wings and catch a glimpse of a smooth white stone shimmering in the sunlight. The faery stones, symbols of hope and companionship, remain hidden treasures. They are waiting to be discovered by those with kind hearts who believe in the enchantment of the butterfly faeries.

Juniors

WENDIGO, OOH, WENDIGO

HONEST LEIGH—AGE
TWELVE, MN.

THE CREATURE ROSE ON ITS HIND LEGS. IT COULD smell something . . . new. Something strange.

And most of all, something tasty. It nipped at the air with its nose, catching and hooking onto the scent of a creature, stronger and more delicious than anything it had ever detected. The Mighty Wendigo would feast on this day!

Satoro whistled a tune as he walked through the thick, prickly brush that some could call a forest. It was annoying, coming all this way to find some dumb creature.

Legend had it that saying Wendigo would summon the beast. Some weird old guy down at the old archway was paying him $150 just to take it down. So, naturally, Satoro chose the logical option.

"Wendigo, oohh Wendigo!" he called out teasingly.

The monster heard something. Something inviting. Someone was calling its name. It almost laughed. This creature is calling him, practically inviting the Wendigo to eat it. It loved the sensation when its name was spoken. The world warped around it, each individual molecule of its body disassembling, only to be reconstructed at another location, drawn to the sound waves of the voice that utters its name.

There it was—the creature foolish enough to summon the creature soon to be responsible for its own demise! Oh, how the beast relished moments like these, when the victim doesn't struggle, oh how wonderful this hunt would b-Wait. Powerful energy was emitted from this creature. The beast examined its prey. It was a normal man, with hair pitch black and eyes the shade of a dying nebula, a purple as pure as light itself! Somehow, someway, this creature, this, this *MAN*, sparked irrational fear in even the mighty Wendigo!

The beast shook off its instincts. Waiting, waiting, for the puny creature's guard to be down. It saw the opportunity. It knew. And it jumped. And the man looked at him.

The Wendigo flew over the man, shocked, startled, and horrified. He flew through the air, crashing through trees older than him, before finally crashing into a hill.

Satoro was walking through a particularly clear patch of forest when he heard a low throbbing noise from behind a bush. For just a second, he swore he could see two red pinpoints of light reflecting from inside the thick undergrowth. He closed his eyes for a second, taking in the splendor from the admittedly overgrown forest, before taking off once again, now in a meditative state of consciousness. Suddenly, there was a sharp crack as a branch snapped behind him. He turned his head, and there it was.

The Wendigo. A slightly humanoid abomination, covered with dark, matted fur, and a deer skull as a head. Satoro's eyes narrowed. Evidently, the creature was surprised to see him staring back, as it missed him completely, traveling around five hundred yards before finally crashing into a sharply inclined hill. There was a large *BOOM* as the forest shook with the impact of this creature.

He sighed.

"Really?" he murmured, his voice echoing with twinges of pity. His thoughts were quickly interrupted by a massive weight knocking him back into a tree. He rebounded on the impact, quickly getting back on his feet. He smiled, a drop of blood dripping from his nose.

"Fine," he told the beast. "We can do this your way."

The Wendigo was shocked. How was this mere human still alive? That blow should have broken every bone in his body, yet it had gotten up like nothing happened. The monster took a step back, putting distance between them. The small human said something.

The Wendigo noticed a glow in the space around the human's hands. It narrowed its eyes, thinking the glow was just an illusion.

Until the man moved, the sheer severity of this small being's speed startled the beast, making it open to attacks. The air whistled as energy manifested into a tangible blade, cutting the air and the Wendigo. The beast staggered back, completely unaware that its own arm had been severed from its body. There was a second of silence, as if reality itself had paused from the swiftness of this attack. Then everything caught up, and the beast flew backwards through a tree, rolling and tumbling its way to a complete stop.

Satoro stared at the limp body of this revered and horrific beast. It was dead. Not moving, breathing, or any signs of life. Inky darkness began to pour out of its eye sockets, staining the ground beneath it. The liquid looked like a hole in reality, absorbing

all light. As he stared in horror, the ink became sharp, tentacle-like appendages, lifting the beast into the air. It slowly began to engulf the Wendigo, covering its entire body until there was nothing left. The severed arm grew back larger and misshapen. The two stared at each other for a moment. Then the shadow-covered beast's head snapped up, and its two small, scarlet eyes glowed like fire at midnight. It lowered itself to the ground, twitching unnaturally. It raised one arm, the air humming with power, as the ground rose into the air, forming an enclosed area.

"Now that's more like it!" exclaimed Satoro. But then, to his shock, the beast uttered something, its voice dark and booming. "You killed me. How?"

Satoro laughed. "Now, why would I tell you?"

"Never mind that. Now, puny human. Prepare to feel"—It let out a blood-curdling screech—"the Wendigo's Eldritch Wrath!"

It lunged at Satoro, claws extended, screeching horribly. He easily sidestepped the blow but was met with an inky black projectile to the stomach, pushing him back, almost making him fall off the edge in the process. Luckily, he regained his balance just as the creature swiped at him. He feigned with a backflip, kicking the head of the beast on the way up. Propelling himself downwards using the momentum of his foot, he kicked, but the creature teleported backwards, rendering his attack worthless.

The Wendigo grabbed him by the neck, then threw him a hundred feet into the sky. Just as he reached the height of his arc, the monster teleported above him, knocking him downwards at an alarming rate with a flurry of punches, kicks, stabs, and slashes.

Suddenly, he reached the ground, crashing into the forest floor at the speed of sound. There was a huge dust explosion, creating a crater the size of a small house, and in the center was Satoro.

The Wendigo stood above him, visually searching for any signs of life. Unsuccessful, the beast made a sharpened blade out of the darkness. Moving to impale the man, it rapidly shoved the blade downwards. Milliseconds before impact, before his life ended, his hand zoomed forward, catching the spear. He opened his eyes. With a tone inspiring regret and fear into the Wendigo, he uttered one word to end it all.

"Enough."

He moved faster than any creature's eyes could see, escaping the beast's hold. He followed up a kick with an arcane explosion, knocking the beast into the air. With eyes glowing brighter than the sun, he teleported to the beast. He simply put his hand on its chest and pushed. The sheer force of the push went straight through the abomination's body.

The Wendigo looked down at itself. There was a hand there, in his chest. Where did that come from? He gasped for breath, but the air seemed to refuse to go into its lungs. It was mad. Why was there no air? Where did the hand in its chest come from? It gurgled, coughing up some dark substance. Then it fell. It was so tired. It wanted to sleep. So much pain. Then suddenly, it did. It went to sleep. It's final sleep. The creature passed the next second.

Satoro floated to the ground. He took in a breath. Summoning all his final strength, he teleported himself back to the archway where he met the man who was paying him. Seeing Satoro alive still, the man knew what had happened.

"Did-did you kill it? The Wendigo?" the small man asked. Satoro barely choked out a yes before falling to the ground. Everything went dark. He fell asleep.

THE WITNESS

MADDISON MILLER—AGE
THIRTEEN, MI.

IT WAS A NORMAL DAY IN MT PLEASANT, MI. Everyone was doing good and having a nice day. Then in class, they started watching the news and heard that there was a mysterious man and woman running around and finding little kids to catch, torture, and kill. Next thing you know, they have to go into lockdown.

They hear footsteps and gun shots, and girls named Lily and Julliea, they start freaking out and Julliea is texting Lily saying, *"Are you ok?"*

Lily doesn't respond. Julliea starts freaking out even more. When the cops come, they catch the bad guy. Sadly, he had shot six people. Julliea doesn't know who they are, but she found out. She was relieved to know Lily wasn't one of them.

The Next Day

Juliea still can't find Lily. She had asked her parents and close friends. Still no luck. A sheriff is trying to find Lily, and they have clues! They found gloves with fingerprints; they're getting the gloves sent to a lab so they can find out who did this.

As they are doing that, Julliea is sitting in silence, thinking about who could do this. They haven't found the body. Two weeks pass by. They should've received the results by now. Julliea goes to the lab and finds out that they never got any labs for a murder in four months. She thinks it's the sheriff trying to keep a secret. The next day, she goes to the sheriff's office. Julliea walks up to the sheriff (her name is Maddie) and she says, 'Why the heck would you do something like that?'

'What did I do?' asks Maddie.

Julliea: "You never went to the lab! How do you explain that because you're acting suspicious?

Maddie: "Okay, listen. I did that because the last time I went, they got it wrong. I don't trust them. But you can trust me. I will find out who did this!"

Julliea: "How do I know I can trust you? What if you lie, you've lied to your co-worker, Sam."

Maddie: "That was because of a family issue. Now leave, it's late, so go get some rest."

Julliea: "Okay, whatever."

After that, she went home and all she could think about was the fact that Maddie had lied before, and she had killed somebody because she is a sheriff. All Maddie could think about was that she just lied and couldn't get it out of her head, and now she hopes Julliea never finds out what happened to Lily. Julliea spends every day going in the woods, around the school, in her own house, and in Lily's. Still no luck. Julie tells herself to think she will find her and she will never stop looking, even if it takes her until she is sixty years old.

One Year Later

· · ·

It's been one year and Julliea sadly can't find Lily anywhere. Maddie keeps getting even more suspicious. Julliea thinks she did it. Next thing you know, Julliea gets a call saying they found a blood trail and are going to follow it and offer for her to come in case it's Lily. Julliea gets in her car and starts driving really fast, she is so nervous. *What if it is Lily? What if it isn't!* She says to herself.

When Julliea gets there, she sees Maddie and Sam, and they walk towards each other. They follow the blood trail. They see the end with a big pile of blood. They see trash bags around the body, and there are flies around them. It smells like human flesh. They walk over and see a knife next to the boy and footprints. None of the footprints are their footprints. They look at the blood and see that it is fresh. They take out a blood test and see how new it is, and the test says the blood is one day old.

The person they found is not Lily. It is the new kid. It seems he stabbed himself before the murderer got to him because some of the footprints are his, but some are not. But what is the blood trail from?

"Maybe he stabbed himself up there by the road, and the murderer dragged him up here?" Sam says.

"No. The murderer walked up behind him and stabbed him through the back twice. Then dragged him over here." Maddie says.

"How do you know?" Sam replies.

"By the way he is lying on the ground and the way the knife is. The shape of the blood trail." Maddie says.

Julliea and Sam get a little confused and think Maddie is being a little creepy, like she knows something. We go home, and I stay at Sam's place. She and I talk about how we think that we can't find the suspect, and yet Maddie is acting kind of suspicious. Julliea and Sam talk for four hours, they don't want to think badly if it isn't her. If it is, they want to and also want to stay away from her. They are thinking of doing a drive-through murder test, yet Maddie won't agree. That gives them more clues to think it is her. Sam tries to ask again, but Maddie grabs her keys and runs out the door like she is going to get caught. Maddie is driving around all night and wasting her money on gas because she knows we're at the sheriff's station.

Sam and Julliea get in their car and follow Maddie to make sure she isn't up to nonsense. Julliea sees Maddie get out of her car and run into the abandoned house that no one dares to go into. When she is entering, she looks around to make sure no one sees her. Little does she know, I saw everything.

Sam and Julliea think to themselves, *why would she be in there?* They follow her in and see she has lit some candles and is sitting in front of them, saying, "Please don't let them find out about what I have done. They would hate me for life. I just felt like hurting one person, and I really did more than just hurt them. I started liking it, so I killed more and more people, leading up to one important person. I wish I could go back in time and not do all of that. Covering for myself is hard, please help me."

We hear everything she says. We also leave the building quietly, going to her car and opening the front doors, all the doors. Finally, we go to the trunk. We see a body in a body wrap. We take it out and run to our car. Throw the body in the car and drive home. We get home and open the body bag, and you won't believe who we found in there, Lily!

I've been looking for her for years, and little did I know, Maddie, the sheriff, killed her. I was right. Maddie killed her and hid her from me when I cried myself to sleep every night because I didn't have my best friend anymore. I run to my room and cry until I fall asleep. The next day, I didn't know what to do. Maddie was loose on the streets, and now I know she's a psycho killer.

In my head, I think, *WE HAVE TO TRAP HER!* So, I start thinking about what the trap will look like and how it will work. Julliea starts thinking really hard because she really wants to try to live a normal life, even without her bestie, not for three years of looking for her and finding out she's dead. Sam was scared to go to work the next day, so she planned on calling in and saying she was sick, but then Maddie would maybe bring something for her to help her feel better, because she always did.

Sam thinks to herself, 'What if she poisons it?' She is scared to do either of them, so she grabs her keys and goes to work, driving terrified the whole way. Then, Sam thinks, 'we could torture her like she tortured all of them.' Sam calls Julliea while she is turning around to go home.

When she arrives, Julliea is already wanting to get started. Sam says, "We have to make a plan first, silly girl."

Julliea, rolls her eyes and replies, "Okay."

They start talking, and they think they have a way, although it is illegal. They really want to do this because Maddie has done far worse. Their plan is to torture Maddie so badly that she is in pain. The worst pain ever, so she was screaming, and no one could hear her.

Julliea asks if she can do it because Maddie killed her bestie, who felt like a sister.

Sam says that's ok, but we need to find the right place for it. They say they should burn down the barn in their backyard. They grab their things, their flare gun, and the tape, some string to hold her hostage. They went to the police station like it was a normal day, but Maddie didn't know it wasn't a normal day. Little did Maddie know, Sam and Julliea are going to trick her. Maddie told them she was going to leave soon, and

Sam and Julliea were going to grab her and tape her mouth shut and toss her in the car, but they wanted to be more professional.

When Maddie was about to leave, Julliea said, "Hey, do you want to go out for dinner tonight?"

Maddie said, "Yeah, that's fine. Why do you want to all of a sudden?"

'We don't know. We just want to eat with you . . ." Julliea says.

They go to dinner, and Sam and Julliea are thinking of asking Maddie to go home with them, and they will set her on fire and make sure she is in pain, just like all the things she did to all the people she murdered. After dinner, they ask Maddie if she wants to come over for a sleepover. Maddie said she is fine with it. They all get in the car and drive home. On the way home, Maddie drives, but Sam and Julliea sit in the back, so they can think of what to do when they trap her. When they arrive home, they all get out and go in, and when they go in, Sam and Julliea shove Maddie into the closet and lock it. Maddie is screaming, asking to be let out.

Maddie: "LET ME OUT"

Sam: "NO! You think it's funny to kill kids and . . . LILY!!!"

Maddie: "Please, I didn't want to."

Julliea: "Then why the heck would you do that? By the way, we're going to make you suffer like you made other kids suffer."

After that, Maddie is screaming, bawling her eyes out, and begging them to let her go. Julliea grabs the gasoline and pours it all over Maddie. Grabs the lighter. Next thing you know, Maddie is getting burned alive in the barn.

She is screaming and saying, "Please let me go. Just let me go, PLEASE."

Sam and Julliea walk out and call the fire department so they don't get into trouble. The cops show up and they made the fire stop. They found the body and told us. We made sure to act upset.

One Week Later

They got a new sheriff in town, and her name is Cat. Sam and Julliea told her everything, and Cat told them that she could keep a secret. After that they all went home and tried to live a happy life.

They always wanted to know why Maddie would do such horrible things, but they never knew. Cat said we should just leave it behind us, and that's hard to do, but we are trying.

We live a happy life and Julliea can go to school again. Sam has her job back, and she owns the sheriff's station. Cat is starting to get the hang of being a sheriff/detective. They all put the past behind them and are trying to forget about it, like Cat told them to. They all live their lives while they can.

NEWS19: "Another murder in town! Who could it be this time?"

THE END

FEAR THE DEEP

GRAYSON MAYWOOD—AGE
THIRTEEN, WA.

In May of 1842, in Columbia, now known as Washington, 14-year-old Raynard Graywood, or for short Ray, sat at his desk plotting his escape.

He was the son of Jonathon Graywood, more commonly known as Captain Gray, the greatest sea captain of the Pacific. His father was going on an exciting exploration voyage to an extensive group of islands west of Skagit, and Ray was told he couldn't come. His mother and father had said it was too dangerous for a kid to go on a journey of that magnitude. But I'm not a child anymore, and I can fight for myself, Ray had thought and expressed to his parents. The sea was the only place he belonged, and he couldn't imagine not partaking in this monumental adventure. That was why he was going to stowaway.

For an hour, Ray was planning in the room he shared with his brother. His brother wasn't around much, as he was often away in the mountains working as a fur trapper. Thinking about what he would bring in his small pack for his expedition, Ray finally settled on his slingshot, clothing, small blanket, journal, rope, and special compass.

His compass had been passed down in the family for generations; it was always passed down to the oldest son, but Ray's brother had not wanted anything to do with it. The noble compass was a dark gray color and had a wolf's head and the name Graywood engraved on the cover. But when opened, the needle was shaped like a feather. The awe-inspiring compass was his most prized possession, and he took it everywhere.

The next morning, Ray set out. The first step was to get up before dawn and sneak onto the Omniscient. The Omniscient was the most magnificent ship on the Pacific Ocean and its surrounding waters. I need to be quick and quiet, Ray thought as he slipped out of his bed. He slowly cracked his door open and silently left his room. He stalked down the hallway as quietly as a mouse. He was tiptoeing when he stepped on a floorboard that creaked. He froze. He heard the soft breathing of his parents sleeping, meaning they hadn't heard him. Hopefully, his mother wouldn't realize that he was gone until the Omniscient had left with Ray on it.

His mother was the nicest, kindest person he had ever met, but Ray thought she was a little overprotective. He opened the front door and tiptoed out into the town. Ray loped past shops, houses, mills, and forges. He was passing the mayor's house, which was the best and most expensive in their town, when he heard a boyish voice that said, "Where are you going?"

Ray quickly spun around to see a boy named Maxwell standing in the doorway of the mayor's house. Ray and Maxwell had a very strange relationship. Maxwell was better fed than Ray, as Maxwell's father did not have to work very hard to make more than Captain Graywood ever would in a year. But Maxwell still tried to be friends with Ray, even though Ray wasn't always nice to him. Maxwell was kind and likable, and would listen to anything Ray would say without interrupting.

"Where are you going!?" said Maxwell again forcefully.

Ray thought about lying to him, but it wouldn't help, so he told him, "I am stowing away on the Omniscient."

Instead of judging him, Maxwell asked, "Can I come too?".

"Absolutely not!" replied Ray with alarm.

"Awww, just bring me back something," he whined.

Ray was thoroughly annoyed. "Fine, just don't tell on me."

"Okay, just don't die".

"I won't, now leave me alone, I can hold my own," Ray replied angrily before stalking off into the night.

Ray boarded the Omniscient and snuck into the lower cargo hold. He sat down and slowly drifted into a light doze. He was woken by the movement of the ship; the creaking of the mahogany wood comforted him.

The slap of the water on the side of the vessel greeted him like an old friend. Ray had been on the water since before he could walk, but had never been on such an important sailing. Ray was about to sneak up to the main deck to see how far from the port they were when he heard a distant BOOM. It echoed across the water, shaking the waves and ringing in Ray's ears. Mere seconds later, a crash sounded from the port side of the Omniscient.

Alarmed, Ray rushed to the main deck, ignoring the stares of the crewmates. In the distance, the figure of a ship floated ominously toward them. It was a group of privateers! Privateers were like pirates, but more interested in taking your supplies than your life. Nevertheless, if they failed to win a fight against them, their trip would come to a sticky end.

Then Ray heard footsteps, heavy footsteps. Just then, the crewmates started to make way for someone, but before they had divided, Ray knew who it was by the crisp captain's hat looming over everyone's heads.

"What are you doing here?" Ray's father bellowed. Ray

looked up at his father's face, expecting to see only fury, but under the weathered features of his face was mostly concern.

"I could not miss out on this!" Ray replied hotly despite being incredibly happy to see his father.

"We have no time, get in the cargo hold!" his father said.

"What!?! No! I can fight!" Ray replied, his voice rising in pitch. The captain could see Ray wasn't going to the cargo hold. His father relented and tossed him a sword.

"If you won't hide, you might as well make yourself useful."

Ray knew the sword wouldn't do anything, but he brandished it with triumph over the fact that the greatest man to sail the seven seas trusted him with a nautical battle! The ship was only about thirty feet away. Suddenly, Ray had an idea. He rushed to the arms rack and grabbed a small knife and a rope. He tied the knife to the end of the rope, creating a crude model of a grappling hook.

Ray went to the bow of the Omniscient, which was shaped like a Thunderbird from Native American folklore. Ray threw the knife at the crow's nest of the other ship. It sank in with a dull THWACK.

He grabbed hold of the rope, sent up a quick prayer, and jumped off the side of the ship.

The first thing Ray saw when he climbed up the side of the raiders' ship was two burly, scar-faced men staring at him with swords raised. Ray had not expected this. One of the men swung his sword at Ray, but Ray parried and sent sparks flying. The sparks hit a pile of gunpowder, causing it to burst into flames. Ray used this diversion to dart in between the privateers and hide behind a storage container of likely stolen goods.

Ray looked up. A storm was brewing. In fact, it wasn't brewing . . . it was in full swing!

The clouds were roaring with thunder. Lightning lit up the

scene, and troubled waves bullied the Omniscient and the raider ship. Ray was glad he didn't have to worry about the privateers; they were busy with the growing fire, but there were other problems.

Right then, an ear-splitting *CRACK* was heard from the starboard side of the raiders' ship, sending Ray flying toward the railing. The hardwood connected with his head, sending a wave of pain through his rapidly swelling skull. He got up and immediately grasped the railing. He was dizzy and his vision was distorted, but he thought he could make out the shape of some type of wriggling tail in the waves, or maybe it was an arm?

Whatever it was, it twisted and convulsed in the water. More somethings hit the boat, more gunshots rang out, and Ray realized the boat was sinking.

"Hurry, Raynard, jump!" Ray's father bellowed amidst the chaos. Ray realized that now was not the time to negotiate with his father. He got a running start and leaped off the bow of the boat. He flew through the air. Suddenly, gravity took over and sent Ray plummeting toward the sea. Ray tried not to panic, and with a steely repose, he whipped out his blade and stuck it in the side of the Omniscient.

The sword sank in with a THUNK, and Ray was left dangling over the disquieted water. Ray was hauled up, patted on the back by the sailors, and scolded by his father. Ray hoped his father's criticism was just a cover for the pride he felt toward Ray. Ray turned around. The once sneaky and silent privateer ship was now up in flames and rapidly being submerged into the raging water. But something more sinister was contributing to the schooner's descent.

Through the steam, he thought he saw glistening black tendrils, ripping at the vessel's rails and cargo. Ray was sure the reaching and grasping figures were tentacles! But no mere squid had as many tentacles as were seemingly unending, reaching out of the toiling expanse of water.

The terrifying truth flooded Ray's mind as he screamed the one thought filling it. "Kraken!"

The rowers were told to row, and the remaining workers were instructed to fight. All about the Omniscient were the talks of being a feast for this giant monster.

Ray was told to hide, but unfortunately, he didn't. Where the raiders' ship had sunk, all that was left was a few pieces of debris and bubbles floating to the ocean's surface.

Everything was ominously quiet, and even the roaring thunder seemed to pause. It was calm before the chaotic storm. Ray stood paralyzed with fear, along with everybody else on the ship. Even the rugged Captain Gray was rendered frozen at the reality of the Kraken attack.

A huge crash shattered the silence, resonating through the ship, signaling the start of a war. Tentacles shot out of the sea and wrapped themselves around everything they could reach. The sailors and Ray slashed at the tentacles, and the moon shone ominously on the glistening deck. Fear crippled Ray's legs, sending him barreling toward the wooden floor. He sat there motionless as he took in the horrific scene playing around him.

At that moment, Ray glimpsed his father in the crowd of sailors. He was fighting gallantly, but there were still too many. Captain Gray was too busy fending off the multitude of tentacles to notice the single tentacle slipping silently toward his back. Ray rushed to his feet and sprinted toward his father, slipping several times on puddles of blood, water, and ink. He reached his father and hastily sliced the tentacle. But as he did that, another tendril whacked him in the back of the head, sending him toppling over onto the floor again.

Ray was about to hop to his feet and storm into the heat of

the battle, but something had already done it for him, and he was dangling over the deck. Ray realized the Kraken had grasped him. The last thing Ray saw was a terrified look in his father's eyes as Ray was plunged into the cold, dark, and unforgiving sea.

The water swallowed Ray, and he sank into the watery depths. The cold snatched his breath, and Ray almost gasped in a lungful of water. Once he recovered from the shock, he started swimming towards the surface. Then he felt something grasp his leg, and he was pushed down farther toward the watery grave waiting for him at the bottom. He looked down and saw a glowing red eye staring up at him. Terror bullied Ray into kicking and flailing. But, alas, it was to no avail.

The horrifying silhouette of the Kraken floated below him, causing Ray's instincts to kick in, and he pulled out his sword and chopped at the tentacles. They let go, and Ray immediately started to swim to the surface, guided by the ominous light of the moon. His lungs screamed for him to breathe, but he did not give in to the urge. He grabbed a board floating in his direction and tagged along on its journey. He broke the surface and looked around. And what alarmed him to a level he did not know possible?

The Omniscient was sinking!

Ray had a terrible decision to make. He could paddle toward the struggling ship and try to help, but the odds were stacked against him. His best chance of survival was to try to swim home and get help. If a group of sailors and their captain couldn't keep the Omniscient afloat, then one more fourteen-year-old would not make any difference. Also, Ray knew his father would not want him to come back.

He looked back once more and watched as the Omniscient was plunged farther into the water, its last groan like a deep, sorrowful cry echoing over the stealing sea.

He heard a voice on the water. "Go, Ray! Go and save yourself!"

The going was easy at first as Ray drifted along the sea at a steady pace. But within a few hours, hunger started to gnaw at his bones, and the events of the past few days washed over him like a raging storm. He found himself wishing that he had listened to his parents and stayed home far from the Kraken. If he had not started the fire, the Kraken would have never come, as legend says that fire is a way to summon the wretched creature.

A suffocating fear of the water and what lay in it started in Ray's soul and grew deeper every time he saw movement in the water. Most of the time, it was just his weary mind playing tricks on him, but sometimes it was a herring or smelt. Ray was able to stab them out of the water, make a small fire on the wet board, and eat it.

This would take the edge off of the hunger clenching his stomach, but would never account for one of his mother's delicious home-cooked meals, steaming gloriously on a plate.

As Ray dreamed of his mother's apple pie, something nearby was also dreaming of a meal. Ray lay on his raft, foaming at the mouth at the thought of his father's famous roasted salmon, unaware of a strange black rock appearing on the horizon.

Suddenly, something bumped the raft and Ray shot up. Tens of tall, black, knife-like fins were circling the raft. He knew he had to stay calm and not move, but fear gripped him and threatened to rip his calm apart. He sat there marveling at the terrifying beauty of the killer whales as they circled and jumped around him. An idea flooded his brain, and he pulled out the rope from the pack and threw it around one of the fins. It immediately started to swim away, dragging him behind.

After an hour, Ray could see land as a dark strip on the

horizon. He was almost there when he decided to cut the orca free and paddle. He patted the orca on the head and cut it free.

"Thank you, my dear friend, I will forever be in your debt," Ray thanked gratefully. Then Ray realized for the first time that the whole pod had stayed with the one killer whale the whole way. It showed that friendship and family are powerful. It gave Ray a meek hope. The hope that his father had survived.

The momentum from the marine creature's push wore off, and Ray had to start paddling as hard as he could toward the details of the land. He decided to have no more breaks and paddle the rest of the way. After nearly an hour, he almost blacked out, an aching hunger bored into his gut, and slicing thirst cut his tongue.

He looked out on the expanse of forbidden water, wishing he could pour the whole ocean down his thirsty throat. His reflection on the sea had sunken cheeks, desperate eyes, and a bloody shoulder. He just had to get to shore.

He jumped off the raft a started to swim to shore. He started strong, but weeks of barely any food or water taxed him, and he could barely stay afloat. He swam a few more minutes before he started to sink. He slowly wafted out of consciousness. He heard a familiar voice and a splash nearby before he took a lung full of water. The last thing he saw was a familiar boyish face.

"I think he's awake!"

"I knew he would!"

"Oh, praise the Lord!"

These were the first things Ray heard as he opened his eyes. He was on the bed in his room, and standing over him were his mother and two other figures that surprised him. It was his brother, William, and Maxwell. William looked a little embarrassed to be there, and Ray knew why. Captain Gray had fought against William's career, and in the end, they would not speak to each other. Maxwell's clothes were dripping wet.

"What are you doing here?" Ray asked Maxwell angrily.

"Don't talk to him like that!" his mother said unexpectedly. "He saved your life!"

"Saved my life?" Ray asked, confused.

Then it hit him: Maxwell had saved him from drowning. Guilt washed over Ray. Ray thought of all the times he had dismissed Maxwell when he was kind to him just because he was different.

"Maxwell, I'm sorry," Ray said.

"It's okay," Maxwell replied.

"No, it isn't. You have always tried to be my friend, and I have been unkind to you."

"Thank you."

Once that was over, another thought came to Ray's mind. And as if by magic, it was answered by a knock on the door. And in stepped Ray's father.

Ignoring the pain he felt in all his body, Ray shot up and wrapped his father in an embrace. After tears were cried and prayers were answered, Ray finally asked the question that had been on his mind since he woke up.

"How did you survive?" Ray asked.

"Well, it is a long story," said Captain Gray. "When you left for help, the crew and I knew the boat had no chance. We made rafts and gathered the food, and we set out for the islands out west. We lost one group to the Kraken, but the rest of us and I got by. We made it to the islands in a week, and once we were there, we immediately started hunting and recharging. The islands were extremely bountiful. We made a ship and sailed it back here." He took a breath and continued.

"You better come see the ship," he gestured for Ray to follow. They all went out to the port and saw the ship. It was crudely made, but it was strangely beautiful. It had a sail of animal furs, and its body was a mix of timbers. But what stood out was the writing on the side of it. It said, *"Raynard, Kraken Master"* in big letters.

"But Father, I didn't do anything to master the Kraken," said Ray.

"Oh, but you did. One of the wooden gunpowder crates exploded in the water, causing the Kraken to be stunned for long enough for me and the crew to get away."

Ray and the rest of the family sat there and discussed the last few weeks and what would happen next. William and Captain Gray even made up.

"Father?" prompted Ray.

"Yes, Raynard?" replied his father.

"Next time, I'll listen to you if you say not to come."

Ray got the whole group to laugh as they stared upon the waters where the Kraken still roamed.

XANDER

SAGE LEIGH—AGE TEN, MN.

It was a sunny day, definitely nothing could go wrong.

While I was buying some bread, after I paid for the bread, the employee stopped me and asked, "What are you?" I stopped at that question, "Uuuuhm, someone in a costume!"

Halloween was 5 months ago said the employee I gotta run. I thought okay, bye! Hey!

Wait! Phew! That was a close one. I should get home now. I should go to bed. BOOM!

Crap! What was that!?

For a second, I noticed something familiar about that sound. It came from the border that the sound woke up the whole neighborhood. I can't go out, so I can fly. I don't care, I burst through the door, used my shadow breath, no one could see me. I ran to the tallest hill that was closest to me, I spread my wings, and jumped. I opened my eyes. I was flying! I could see the whole town from here, but something was off. It got darker the closer I got to Lake Superior. I went closer, BOOM, there it is again! I knew something was off. A huge wave of water flew above me. Well great. What a nice time for a shower. I said sarcastically.

Sploosh! Well, that was cold, I said. I better head back down. As I got back down, I searched for shelter. I saw a broken shed, well, that will do. First, I searched for supplies. I found 3 cans of tuna. What monsters do this to dolphins? 9 mushrooms 7 potatoes. The best spot to sleep was a rock. The next morning, I was thinking of my pet rock, Dwayne The Rock Johnson. Right before I left, something shiny caught my eye. A phone cracked. I pressed on it. Something turned on. It sounded like this I just wanna tell you how I'm feeling, gotta make you understand, never gonna give you up. Hehehehe I just got rickrolled. I forgot I gotta go, but something else was in here with me. As soon as I saw it, I instantly knew what it was: the evil mage. Puny dragonborn, you will never defeat me, you will die like your idiot friends! What did you just say? I cast fire ball! Hehehe counterspell! OOF! Eat this! I said. Magic missiles! Ow! Scorching ray! Ssssss! Ow! I call these buck chuckets. Clang! Stone fists! Clang boom slash! I summon chicken jockey! Heh, fairie fire! Sssssssssss! Spare me, please. No. The tree elves will keep you in prison forever.

Thanks for reading Quest of Xander! Hope you enjoyed reading!

THE SALMON BERRY DRAGON

LILY TUCKER—AGE 7, WA.

(This story is written in Lily's words. Since she is seven and can barely write, let alone type, I copied it here for her.)

WHEN WE GO HIKING IN THE SUMMER, THE SALMON berries are always gone before we get there.

That's because the Salmon Berry Dragon gets up earlier than we do. It lives deep in the forest and comes out when the berries are ready to eat. It's green with pink frills and is the same size as a big cat tree. Its tail splits like the cucumber plant I tried to grow in a pot by the window.

It walks through the woods, eating all the berries. It doesn't leave any for anyone else. Why would it? It's a dragon. The Salmon Berry Dragon. The berries are his, anyway.

It's real. I've never seen it, but that's because it's so good at hiding, but I promise it's real. That's why there are no salmon berries left when we go hiking—the end.

AUTHOR BIOGRAPHIES

B.E. Padgett:

B.E. Padgett is a YA and children's author from the Pacific Northwest. Before pursuing her passion for writing and storytelling, she worked as a student affairs professional in higher education. She graduated with a bachelor's degree in English from Central Washington University. She is an avid tea drinker and loving auntie. She is best known for her middle-grade fantasy series The Reeds of West Hills.

Jensen Reed:

Jensen Reed is a multi-genre short story author who loves feeding characters to zombies and making readers cry. Residing in Minnestoa with her family of four, cats, and reptiles, she enjoys writing, reading, painting, and crochet. You can find her at beacons.ai/AuthorJensenReed

Cory Laniewski:

My name is Cory Laniewski. I am a thirty-one-year-old author, released my debut novel, *"Before the Shadows"* in 2024, and have been writing short stories for some time. I am a chef, and I hope to continue writing as a part-time job.

I've two cats, a wife, and I enjoy board games. This short story is written with historical details about the Archbald Pothole State Park in Pennsylvania, home to the world's largest pothole. It is a fictionalized take on the pothole, and the story is suspense fiction.

Robin Jeffrey:

Robin Jeffrey was born in Cheyenne, Wyoming, to a psychologist and a librarian, giving her a love of literature and a consuming interest in the inner workings of people's minds, which have served her well as she pursues a writing career. She currently lives happily with her husband and their out-of-control comic book collection in the PNW. She is the author of the urban fantasy series The Night, as well as the author of the sci-fi mystery series The Cadence Turing Mysteries. When not writing, Robin loves sharing what she's learned about the craft and business of writing in workshops both online and in person. (https://robinjeffreyauthor.com/)

Breanna Dawn:

Breanna Dawn is a writer and creative who is based out of Indiana with her husband, David, and daughter, Olivia, and their two fur babies. Breanna spends most of her days gaming, reading, and making memories with her family. You can always find her with an iced coffee, a journal, and a pen.

Liz Sullivan-Fisk

Raised in Granite Falls, WA, Liz enjoys hiking the plentiful trails in the area and just sitting back to read a good book with whichever one of her four cats decides to claim her lap in that instant. She survives on coffee and enjoys a good, rainy day. She also enjoys crafting and baking. She lives in Granite with her husband, four cats (Ollie, Helena, Lester, and Alex), dog (Eevee), and horse (Strider).

Lucas Jankovic:

Lucas Jankovic is a private investigator and writer living in Arlington, Washington. In his free time he enjoys camping, as well as spending time with his wife Chloe Rae.

Kelly Crumpley:

Kelly is the author of adult fiction and children's books, the *Monarch Empirium* Fantasy Series, and *Mermaid ABCs* with her original watercolor illustrations. When she's not fueling her creative endeavors with far too much coffee or crunching on apples like a true Seattleite, you'll find her exploring the trails of the Pacific Northwest, her three loyal sidekicks—Blueberry, Maple, and Mochi—trotting alongside her. Reading, writing, and painting are the lifeblood of her days, filling quiet moments with vivid stories and splashes of color. She lives with her husband and son, who graciously tolerate the ever-growing stacks of books and art supplies that seem to multiply overnight.

Brittany Tucker

Brittany Tucker is the author of several whimsical fantasy series that cater to readers of all ages, from middle-grade to adult. She also co-authored a story-plotting workbook designed for tweens and teens.
She owns First Fruit Press, an assisted indie publishing service

dedicated to helping writers bring their stories to life. Brittany frequently teaches writing classes and workshops suitable for all skill levels in her community. She resides on an island off the coast of Washington with her family, cats, and ball pythons.

Sara Mosier:

Sara A. Mosier is a Nebraska author and poet. When she's not conversing with her repertoire of haunted antique dolls, she's writing down all the dark and beautiful things she's wanted to see in literature since she was fourteen.

Her debut novel "Lithium" a queer paranormal romance can be found on Amazon and Etsy. Also, her collection of typewriter poetry is titled "Unfettered: A Collection of Poetry." Both are available in multiple formats on Amazon, and printed, signed copies are available on Etsy. Her collection of lgbtq novellas is available now on Inkspired: "Spectral Ties," A dark vampire story with horror elements, "Shades of Red," a dramatic romance, "A Thousand Years," a historical 1920s romance, and "Love for Sale," another paranormal romance.

Honest Leigh:

Honest is a twelve-year-old, previously published author, bibliophile, and gamer, from Minnesota. He enjoys fantasy stories and games like *Breath of the Wild, Minecraft, and Spider-Man 2*. When he isn't reading, you can find him playing football and basketball or creating science experiments.

Maddison Miller:

Maddison Miller is thirteen and has an amazing, supportive family. It consists of brothers and sisters—whole and foster—

her mom and famous stepdad, her dad and stepmom, a little mini farm, and a crazy cat named Bacon. Maddison sings, plays volleyball, and is a certified babysitter. Much love from Michigan!

Grayson Maywood:

Grayson Maywood is thirteen years old and lives with his family on Camano Island, Washington. His hobbies are writing, running, reading, and studying birds!

Sage Leigh:

Sage Leigh is ten years old. He loves video games, reading, and being outside.

Lily Tucker

Lily Tucker is seven years old and spends her days drawing dragons, playing with dragons, and imagining all the ways she could *be* a dragon.

ABOUT THE EDITOR

Brittany Tucker is the author of several whimsical fantasy series that cater to readers of all ages, from middle-grade to adult. She also co-authored a story-plotting workbook designed for tweens and teens. She owns First Fruit Press, an assisted indie publishing service dedicated to helping writers bring their stories to life. Brittany frequently teaches writing classes and workshops suitable for all skill levels in her community. She resides on an island off the coast of Washington with her family, cats, and ball pythons.